Mrs Burton Harrison

Short Comedies for Amateur Players

As Given at the Madison Square and Lyceum Theatres, New York...

Mrs Burton Harrison

Short Comedies for Amateur Players
As Given at the Madison Square and Lyceum Theatres, New York...

ISBN/EAN: 9783744784726

Printed in Europe, USA, Canada, Australia, Japan

Cover: Foto ©Andreas Hilbeck / pixelio.de

More available books at **www.hansebooks.com**

SHORT COMEDIES

FOR AMATEUR PLAYERS

AS GIVEN AT THE
MADISON SQUARE AND LYCEUM THEATRES, NEW YORK
BY AMATEURS

ADAPTED AND ARRANGED BY
MRS. BURTON HARRISON

———

ILLUSTRATED BY KELLY

NEW YORK
THE DE WITT PUBLISHING HOUSE

CONTENTS

	PAGE
THE MOUSE-TRAP	1
WEEPING WIVES	15
BEHIND A CURTAIN	47
TEA AT FOUR O'CLOCK	53
TWO STRINGS TO HER BOW	83

The five short comedies selected for this volume are easily within the scope of intelligent amateurs. They have been tested and approved as suitable for this purpose by various audiences assembled in private houses, and by the larger hearing accorded on the occasions noted with each play. In preparing for amateur use these English versions of French originals, I was inspired by a desire to furnish something in which my players might have the benefit of an untrodden field, and be spared comparison with professional predecessors. Few amateur aspirants bear in mind that, in selecting for performance the established dramas identified with the names of artists who have successfully interpreted them, they are exposing themselves to a two-edged sword of criticism. It is manifestly more easy for untried actors to hold the attention of their audience during one act, in which a situation is worked out to its climax, than to deserve continued notice during three or four acts of a long play. The aid derived from quick changes of character, scenery, and costume, in varying the programme, is a great resource for amateurs. And for those reasons I have frequently provided for one entertainment a series, consisting of a monologue and several comediettas, tableaux or acted ballads in succession.

In all "private" theatricals there are three things which cannot be too strongly recommended: (1) The choice of a stage-manager, who shall be absolute ; (2) repeated and faithful rehearsals, and (3) *such previous preparation of the stage as shall insure promptness in the changes. The proverbially long waits of amateur performances are a blight from which the spirits of the audience are slow to recover, whatever the following attraction.*

Most amateurs should put their faith in graceful stage grouping and effective tableaux. These cover a multitude of sins, and may best be relied on by the untried aspirant, together with Hamlet's "forest of feathers, and two provincial roses in his razed shoes," to "get him a fellowship in a cry of players." I have found that simple dances, sometimes introducing volunteers not cast for the play, are, when possible, desirable at the end of a performance. When, for instance, "Two Strings to Her Bow" was first given in Sedgwick Hall, at Lenox, Massachusetts, a calcium light in the gallery, thrown in various tints upon a rustic dance of beautiful young girls grouped in an out-door scene, made an effect as charming as anything I remember on the stage. The same idea was realized at the performance of the same play by amateurs at the Lyceum Theatre, New York.

It is only fair to add that none of these comedies have been given without the benefit of suggestions for the play and training of the players by Mr. David Belasco, to whom as a stage-manager so many of the most successful amateurs in New York have been indebted for his faithful endeavors to develop their possibilities.   C. C. H.

New York, February, 1889.

THE MOUSE-TRAP

A PREDICAMENT

CHARACTERS

MRS. PRETTIPET,
Young Widow.

MORTIMER BRIEFBAG,
Counsellor-at-Law.

THE MOUSE-TRAP was first played in August, 1886, at the Sea Urchins, Bar Harbor. It was repeated at matinées of amateur theatricals, given for the Island Mission and other charities, January 13th and 14th, 1887, at the Madison Square Theatre in New York, when Miss Elsie de Wolfe played Mrs.

Prettipet, Mr. Edward Fales Coward, Mr. Briefbag. This comedietta requires but one interior scene, with a practicable window facing audience. Both characters wear modern morning dress. As "patter" parts, the lines committed to Mrs. Prettipet and Mr. Briefbag should be spoken rapidly and with spirit.

THE MOUSE-TRAP.

*(The scene is the parlor of a flat ; facing audience a win-
dow, practicable, C. ; sofa, work-table, fireplace R.,
door L., two arm-chairs.)*

*(As the curtain rises, Mrs. Prettipet comes running
through door L. in great excitement. In her arms she
holds a basket of crewel-work and wools, which she
throws upon the table, then closes and tries to lock door,
finds key gone, pushes chair against door, sharply
calls off.)*

MRS. PRETTIPET. — Bridget, call Ann and Susan and the
janitor and the elevator-boy. Let everybody look every-
where. Search the entries and the dining-room, the closets
and the coal-scuttle. Secure that wretch you must, dead
or alive. Don't try to open this door, do you hear ? *No
one shall open this door* — if I have to stay here without food
or drink for a week. There's no knowing whether the
monster would n't try to follow me. If I saw him I should

certainly go mad. *(Sits upon sofa, panting.)* Oh, I can't
get over it. The shock was terrible. There I sat calmly
doing my crewel-work beside my bedroom fire, and when
I put my hand out to reach my work-basket — horrors!
he sprang at me! he touched me! All was dark before
me! And that agent swore there was not a drawback to
this flat! He even grazed me with his terrible long tail! I
mean the mouse!

After this I'll go to housekeeping in a balloon. And to-
day, of all days, when I am expecting a call from Mr.
Mortimer Briefbag, my would-be husband. That infatu-
ated young man saw me last summer on the boat for Mount
Desert, was introduced to me upon the pier, pursued me in
a buckboard to find out my hotel, sprained his ankle climbing after me upon the rocks, and capsized three times in
one day learning to manage a canoe that he might take me
out. Since then he's been proposing to me at intervals of
three weeks regularly. He doesn't mind refusals in the least.

I wonder if Mr. Briefbag is afraid of mice. Mr. Prettipet was. Poor Mr. Prettipet, it was his only weakness.
(Handkerchief to eyes.) Of course I shall never marry again.
If I did, it would be only to find a protector. It is hard for
a woman to tread the path of life alone.

(Bridget's voice, outside.) — Misthress Prettipet.

MRS. PRETTIPET. — Have they caught him ?

(Bridget's voice, outside.) — Shure it's a jintleman.

MRS. PRETTIPET. — In the mouse-trap ?

(Bridget's voice, outside.) — He's afther starting up the
steps, and here's his card.

MRS. PRETTIPET *(excitedly)*. — Don't open the door! Don't
open the door, for Heaven's sake! Poke the card under.
(She stoops, takes card from floor, and reads it.) As I sup-
posed — the faithful Briefbag! *(Adjusts her hair and dress
before the mirror.)* Bridget.

(Bridget's voice.) — Yes, mum.

MRS. PRETTIPET.— Tell the gentleman that the key of the drawing-room door is broken in the lock, and we 've sent to fetch a locksmith. Ask him if he 'd mind climbing up the fire-escape. Briefbag will do it. He 's the most obliging soul alive. Besides, it 's only the third floor. *(Goes to window, parts curtains, opens window, and looks down.)* Goodness! there he is in the yard below, attended by the janitor with a ladder. He 's going to try it. Romeo on a fire-escape — ha! ha! ha! Here he comes, climbing as nimbly as a cat. Oh, dear! I wish he were a cat! Hand over hand! How funny a man looks coming up a fire-escape with a high hat and umbrella. Ah, he 's here. Take care, dear Mr. Briefbag. Don't fall, I beg of you. For my sake, don't dash your brains out.

BRIEFBAG *(without).*— Don't speak of it. Perfectly safe, I assure you. Only too happy to come to the rescue of beauty in distress. *(Appearing at window.)* Mrs. Prettipet, good-morning.

MRS. PRETTIPET.— My heart was in my mouth.

BRIEFBAG *(mopping his brow).*— So was mine, to tell the honest truth. I 'm rather out of practice in gymnastics. Besides, it 's a trifle depressing to have all the neighbors' maid-servants gazing at one over the clothes-lines, and the wet things flapping around one's legs.

MRS. PRETTIPET.— Come inside — it 's so dreadfully conspicuous.

BRIEFBAG *(putting one leg over sill).*— Thanks. If it 's all the same to you, I 'll accept your invitation by degrees. *(Fans himself with hat.)*

MRS. PRETTIPET.— This is so very kind of you.

BRIEFBAG *(putting other leg over sill).*— Again, don't mention it. The crisis called for action; and, in the service of the fair, Mortimer Briefbag, attorney and counsellor-at-law, was never known to — ah — in point of fact — to funk.

MRS. PRETTIPET (coquettishly).— Think what would have become of me, had you not climbed to my relief.

BRIEFBAG. — Bewitching widow. Where would I not aspire to climb? Trinity Church steeple would be a mere morning stroll to me, did I but find you at the top.

MRS. PRETTIPET (aside).— A declaration on the window-sill! The man's incurable. (Aloud.) Take care of your umbrella.

BRIEFBAG (slipping into room).— It's all right, thank you. Rain or shine, I've carried that umbrella since I was first called to the New York bar. Such a little matter as climbing up a fire-escape isn't likely to part us now. Loveliest of Letitias, confide to me your sorrows.

MRS. PRETTIPET.— Such a shock! It's too dreadful to mention. Don't speak of it. Take a chair. It's all that agent's fault.

BRIEFBAG.— Go on, go on; what has happened? Speak.

MRS. PRETTIPET.— When I think of it I want to go into hysterics. He—he—he—I—I—I—it—it—it— Oh, Mr. Briefbag, I'm so thankful you are here.

BRIEFBAG.— Tears, Letitia? Allow me to stanch them.

(Fumbles in pocket; takes out law-paper, keys, pipe, etc., fails to find handkerchief, looks distractedly at umbrella, gives that up, seizes a tidy from a chair-back, and wipes widow's eyes. Mrs. Prettipet's hysterics gradually subside.)

(Anxiously.)—There, now, you are better; tell me all about it.

MRS. PRETTIPET (rejecting the arm he attempts to put around her waist).— Mr. Briefbag, I'm astonished!

BRIEFBAG (aside).— I have it. Her modesty has taken alarm at finding herself locked in alone with me. (Aloud.) Shrinking Letitia, do not fear. Say but the word, and without waiting for that confounded locksmith I'll break the door down.

Mrs. Prettipet *(shrieks).*—Oh! don't do that, for good-ness sake; don't think of it! *(Restrains him.)*

Briefbag *(aside).*—What the dickens can it be?

Mrs. Prettipet *(with a strong effort).*—The locksmith will be here very soon. In the mean time let us make the best of it. Now that you are with me, what have I to fear?

Briefbag *(aside).*—She is evidently melting. *(Aloud.)* Dearest Mrs. Prettipet, it is impossible for me to restrain the words of love that bubble from my heart. Believe that I return, ten thousand fold, the sweet sentiments you have avowed for me. Believe——

Mrs. Prettipet *(draws back).*—Again, Mr. Briefbag! You forget yourself.

Briefbag.—Be not so coy.

Mrs. Prettipet *(haughtily).*—Sir, you are presumptuous!

Briefbag *(stiffly).*—In that case, madam, you will permit me to retire. *(Picks up hat and umbrella.)*

Mrs. Prettipet *(wildly, aside).*—Go, and leave me to the mercy of that fiend? *(Aloud.)* Stay, Mr. Briefbag. Can't you understand that my nerves are shattered?

Briefbag *(relenting, aside).*—Timid little creature. *(Aloud.)* Beautiful Letitia, at your command I submit to anything. Do with me what you will.

Mrs. Prettipet *(aside).*—Didn't I hear something scratching? At any price, I'll keep him. *(Aloud.)* It is rare, Mr. Briefbag, that in this calculating world one meets a spirit so sympathetic as your own. *(Aside.)* There, I knew it! It *is* scratching.

Briefbag *(aside).*—Her emotion overcomes her; she grows red, then pale. *(Aloud.)* Trust in me, loveliest Letty. For your sake I would dare any danger, welcome any fate, scale mountains, wade torrents, beard lions in their lair. *(Falls upon his knees.)*

(Bridget's voice. outside.)—Misthress Prettipet.

MRS. PRETTIPET.— Well, Bridget?

(Bridget's voice.) — Sure and the cat's afther catching him. I saw her wid me eyes, and the crathur in her mouth.

MRS. PRETTIPET.— Saved, saved! Thank Heaven! *(She runs to door, opens it, and goes out.)*

BRIEFBAG *(getting up from knees, bewildered).*— What an extraordinary female! Leaving me on my knees, in the middle of a burning declaration, she whisks out of a door which she has previously declared to be inviolably closed, for the purpose of looking at her cat with a crathur in its mouth! And why — why should she thank Heaven?

MRS. PRETTIPET *(running in).*— A frightful disappointment. That stupid Bridget! She can't swear it is not a ball of crewel puss holds in her claws. Before I'm a moment older I'll be sure. *(Sits at table, takes wool-basket, begins to count balls of crewel.)*

BRIEFBAG *(aside).* — Eccentric personage. *(Aloud.)* Ahem!

MRS. PRETTIPET *(counts balls).*— Four — six — eight ——

BRIEFBAG *(aside).*— She ignores me. *(Aloud.)* Madam, I wish you a good-day.

MRS. PRETTIPET *(nervously).*—Going? Oh, no! Mr. Briefbag, you can't go yet. Eight — ten — I shall soon know the worst.

BRIEFBAG.— Madam, your indifference ——

MRS. PRETTIPET.—Mr. Briefbag, you men are so impetuous, so sensitive. Forgive me. From my cradle I was deemed original. Don't go!

BRIEFBAG.—I can't bear to refuse a woman what she's set her heart on. I'll stay.

MRS. PRETTIPET.— Sit right down there on the sofa, and make yourself agreeable, while I count my wools. Tell me something nice and dreadful. *(Aside.)* Oh! anything to while away these moments of suspense. *(Goes on counting.)* Twelve — thirteen ——

BRIEFBAG *(sits on sofa).* — Nice and dreadful! What shall it be?

MRS. PRETTIPET. — Fourteen — sixteen — Let 's talk about wild beasts.

BRIEFBAG *(aside).* — Wild beasts! I 've always taken particular good care to keep them at a distance. *(Aloud.)* A man who has lived a life of adventure, a reckless, daring fellow like myself, has naturally many little episodes more or less exciting. Perhaps I may recall one which was almost — not quite — tragic.

MRS. PRETTIPET. — Twenty-six — twenty-eight — Oh, yes; exactly. Something not quite tragic, but almost.

BRIEFBAG. — Be calm, dear lady; I survived it. I could wish that the incident had occurred in a foreign country, but it did not. It was at Peoria, Illinois.

MRS. PRETTIPET. — Ah, yes. Peoria, Illinois. *(Aside.)* I 'm getting to the end.

BRIEFBAG *(aside).* — Behold her growing agitation. At the very thought of my danger she palpitates. And now, Mortimer, summon up all your eloquence. Consider her a jury that you 're addressing. *(Aloud.)* It might, as I said before, have sounded better had the scene of my narration been laid in some impenetrable forest of the Torrid Zone, or upon Afric's glowing sands. So I should have preferred it, had the animal I was called on to encounter been altogether wild. But she was n't. The affair happened, in point of fact, in a menagerie. Just at the moment when the public within the inclosure had their eyes focused upon a man-fly, walking in an unpleasant attitude across the ceiling, a terrible roaring was heard. Something had evidently broken loose. Nobody stopped to find out what it was. The crowd surged madly in the direction of the doorway. I, unfortunately, was the hindmost. Turning, I beheld an enormous lioness charging full upon me. Quick as thought I opened my umbrella ——

(He opens umbrella. At this moment a mouse springs from Mrs. Prettipet's basket, crosses her lap, and runs across the floor.)

MRS. PRETTIPET.— The mouse ! !

(Mrs. P. utters a piercing shriek, and faints. Briefbag turns, closing and dropping umbrella.)

BRIEFBAG.— Great Heavens, she is fainting ! Look up, Letitia, my adored ; your Briefbag lives — safe, unharmed. *(He slaps her hands, lays her on sofa, dances about her excitedly.)* She's cold and lifeless still. Letitia, believe me, it never really happened! No, she hears me not. . . . Darling, forgive me. I thought you were a jury. Oh, if she would but speak ! My fatal gift of eloquence ; this time it has undone me ! Letitia, do you think a cold key down your back — help, help, water — I must have water. *(He runs out of door.)*

MRS. PRETTIPET *(reviving).*— Where am I ? Ah, I remember now. Mr. Briefbag! Gone! He has left me to my fate. Oh, I cannot stay alone. Suppose it got upon my skirts. Oh, I see it underneath the curtain. I see its tail wag. Help, help, or I shall die !

(She springs up on chair, gathering her skirts tight about her. Enter Briefbag, holding a large plated water-pitcher in his hand.)

BRIEFBAG.— Great Heavens! She's gone mad!

MRS. PRETTIPET.— Save me, save me, Mr. Briefbag !

BRIEFBAG *(putting chair between them).*— Madam, you may rely on me.

MRS. PRETTIPET.— You are a brave man — a hero !

BRIEFBAG.— I — Well, yes, certainly — *(He regains possession of his umbrella.)*

MRS. PRETTIPET.— You who have faced a lioness undaunted.

BRIEFBAG.— Yes, of course I have. *(Aside.)* I 'm glad she did n't hear me say I made that story up.

Mrs. Prettipet.—Then prepare yourself.

Briefbag.— I — I 'm prepared. *(Aside.)* Devil take it, the woman 's lost her wits.

Mrs. Prettipet.—For my sake *(à la Fanny Davenport, in Fedora)*, kill him! kill him!

Briefbag *(aside)*.— Great Scott! Mad as a March hare!

Mrs. Prettipet *(hysterically)*.—It *was* my crewel puss had in her claws.

Briefbag.—Who had in her claws? *(Aside.)* Poor soul, this is terrible.

Mrs. Prettipet.—There he is again—I saw him. Mr. Briefbag, if you love me ——

Briefbag.— What — where — who?

Mrs. Prettipet.— Under your chair.

> *(Briefbag jumps to one side, then stoops, making lunges under chair with umbrella.)*

Mrs. Prettipet.— Until I see him dead before me, I can never leave this chair. There! I see his tail.

Briefbag.— In Heaven's name, whose tail?

Mrs. Prettipet *(distractedly)*.—How often must I tell you? That horrid, horrid mouse!!!

Briefbag *(jumping on other chair)*.—A mouse! No! Where — where — where?

Mrs. Prettipet.— What! you afraid of him?

Briefbag.— My dear madam, believe me, I would cheerfully live with crocodiles, eat all my meals in a den of tigers, sleep with a rhinoceros for my bed-fellow, if it would afford you the slightest satisfaction. But if upon earth there lives an animal that completely chills the marrow of my bones, it is a mouse.

Mrs. Prettipet.—This is dreadful! What shall we do?

Briefbag.—Could n't we call the maids?

Mrs. Prettipet.—They 're all in the kitchen, at the other side of the flat. Could n't you summon up courage to get down to fetch a broomstick?

BRIEFBAG.— Madam, if you were to offer me a seat upon the Bench of the Supreme Court at this minute, I should be utterly unable to stir hand or foot to take it. I am completely paralyzed.

MRS. PRETTIPET.— There; he's run under the fender. Now's your chance.

BRIEFBAG.— Are you quite certain ?

MRS. PRETTIPET.— No, no; he is running up the curtain.

BRIEFBAG *(taking drink out of water-pitcher)*.— Make up your mind, please; it's very wearing.

MRS. PRETTIPET.— Mr. Briefbag, you have asked my hand in marriage. If you rid me of this, our common enemy, 't is yours.

BRIEFBAG.— I have no words in which to frame my gratitude; my feelings overpower me. To wed you has long been the dearest wish of my heart; but I know myself, and if I came into but momentary contact with that creature, I should die upon the spot.

MRS. PRETTIPET.— Then, oh! what shall we do ? Perhaps you could poke the door open with your umbrella.

BRIEFBAG.— A capital idea. *(He leans over, puts down pitcher, and pushes door open.)*

MRS. PRETTIPET.— Bravo ! Now, let us throw things. *(She throws her basket, wools, etc., which hit B.; he dodges in vain.)*

BRIEFBAG *(puts up umbrella to shield himself)*.— A flat failure! Now's my turn. *(Opens and shuts umbrella.)* That's no go.

MRS. PRETTIPET.— Let's make all the noise we can, both together. *(Duet of roars, groans, and hisses.)*

BRIEFBAG.— That mouse is positively Spartan. Stop; I've an idea. I once had some success in my imitations of a cat. *(Makes a terrible caterwauling. The mouse darts from under curtain and out at door.)*

MRS. PRETTIPET *(jumps down, claps hands)*.— There he

goes. Victory, victory; our enemy has fled. (*Slams the door.*)

BRIEFBAG (*getting down, stiff in joints*).— Was n't it Buffon who undertook to say that animal instinct can never be deceived? And that creature mistook me for a *cat*? Disgusting!

MRS. PRETTIPET.— Under the present circumstances, I should prefer one cat to six men, even if they were all heroes like yourself, Mr. Briefbag. Ha! ha! ha!

BRIEFBAG.— That's just like a woman. Use a man, play on his finest feelings, then cast him off.

MRS. PRETTIPET.— You cast *me* off. Did n't you just refuse my heart and hand?

BRIEFBAG.— That, madam, was my misfortune, not my fault. But, rather than remain to afford food for unfeeling merriment, I will take my leave. (*Takes up hat and umbrella ; goes toward door. Quick movement from Mrs. P.*)

MRS. PRETTIPET (*rapidly*).— Oh, don't open that door! I won't hear of it.

BRIEFBAG (*walking to window, looks out*).— Well, although the method offers certain objections, and he's taken away the ladder, I suppose I *can* go as I came. True, I must tell you that on looking down from a great height I am subject to fits of vertigo. If I dash my brains out, do not be surprised. Good-morning!

MRS. PRETTIPET (*holding to his coat*).— Don't go through the window. I'll not hear of it.

BRIEFBAG.— A compound fracture and a lingering illness. There's a good hospital around the corner, and the ambulance *may* come within an hour. Good-day!

MRS. PRETTIPET (*beseechingly*).— Mr. Briefbag!

BRIEFBAG.— Internal injuries; perhaps a hemorrhage.

MRS. PRETTIPET.— Mortimer, for my sake, stay!

BRIEFBAG (*aside*).— She calls me Mortimer! 'T is the music of the spheres! (*Aloud.*) I relent. I'll not go down the fire-escape. I decline to dash my brains out. I renounce the compound fracture. I scorn the hemorrhage.

Mrs. Prettipet *(holds out hand).*— And you 'll take this in their stead ?

Briefbag.— Beauteous and beloved Letitia. Mine at last !

(Bridget's voice outside.) — Sure, and it 's puss that 's got him this time, sure enough. You can say her for yerself, sittin' quite comfortable and atin' him atop the cool-scuttle.

Briefbag.— So perish all our foes. And now, my dear Mrs. Briefbag that is to be, when shall we go to housekeeping ?

Mrs. Prettipet.— When you shall have bought yourself a mouse-trap !

"WEEPING WIVES"

A COMEDIETTA
FROM THE FRENCH OF MM. SIRAUDIN
AND LAMBERT THIBOUST

CHARACTERS:

M. CHAMBLY, . . { *Who has confided to his wife the key of his secretary.*

DELPHINE, . . . { *His wife, who wishes to restrain her husband's love of play.*

ALBERT DE RIEUX, . *Upon his honeymoon journey.*

CLOTILDE, . . . { *His bride, who is studying the idiosyncrasies of mankind.*

JEAN, ... *A servant at the Hotel.*

WEEPING WIVES was prepared at the request of Mr. George Riddle, for his readings, and has been repeatedly acted by amateurs. It is best known through the interpretation of Mrs. Oliver Sumner Teall as Delphine, Miss Alice Lawrence as Clotilde, Mr. Edward Fales Coward as Chambly, Mr. Evert Wendell as Albert de Rieux, and Mr. William Francis Johnson as Jean. With this cast it was included in the programme of the opening night of the Tuxedo Club Theatre, October 25th, 1886; and

was seen at the residence of Mrs. Arthur Murray Dodge, for the benefit of a Day Nursery, March 19th, 1885. It was also given by the same players at Orange, N. J., and elsewhere. At the matinées for the Island Mission, etc., at the Madison Square Theatre, the part of Albert de Rieux was kindly assumed by Mr. Walden Ramsay of the Madison Square Theatre. This comedy demands one scene, the interior of a hotel sitting-room at Baden, with exits R., L., and C.; and the characters wear modern morning dress.

WEEPING WIVES.

ACT I.

SCENE: *Baden, at the height of the fashionable season. The Hotel Parlor. Chambly alone.*

CHAMBLY *(meditating).*—The double zero! Again my ill-luck follows me. Ah, I can't understand it. It is enough to weaken the brain of any man ——

JEAN *(appearing suddenly).*—Monsieur called for me?

CHAMBLY.—No; leave me alone!

JEAN.—Monsieur seems a little put out about something.

CHAMBLY.— Put out! I should think I am. That infernal double zero! There — get along with you, fellow.

JEAN *(with an air of incredulity).* — It can't be that monsieur has been playing?

CHAMBLY.—Hold your tongue, and begone!

JEAN *(sympathetically).*— I am really surprised! Monsieur, then, *has* been playing.

CHAMBLY.— If you breathe a word about my — my unfortunate double zero, to anybody living, you rascal, I 'll — I 'll kidnap you. I 'll drag you to Carlsruhe, and without an attempt at a pretext I 'll throw you neck and heels into the Rhine. Go!

JEAN.— It is n't necessary for monsieur to be so positive — I 'm off, monsieur, this minute. *(Exit Jean.)*

CHAMBLY.— And here I am, with forty-five thousand louis of rent upon my books, and not twenty francs in my pocket. So much for the misguided enthusiasm of a man in his honeymoon. So much for having said to Madame Chambly in my first moment of marital expansion, "Take the key of my secretary, my beloved. From this moment you are the keeper of our fortunes — the disposer of my purse." Strange to say, she accepted. *(Enter Delphine.)* At that time it made little difference. We were not at Baden, and this passion for play had not taken hold of me.

DELPHINE.— "This passion for play?" Monsieur Chambly, what is this I hear? Did we not agree that naughty word should never be mentioned in my presence while at Baden?

CHAMBLY.— I beg pardon, my dear. I was reflecting upon some of the peculiarities of the town. By the way, Baden is a very expensive place, is n't it? You could n't let me have five hundred francs toward current expenses this morning, could you, my love?

DELPHINE.— Would n't that be a little dangerous — considering the peculiarities of the town, my love?

CHAMBLY *(aside).*— She 's too clever by half, confound it!

DELPHINE *(sits, showing key of secretary).*— No, Monsieur Chambly; when I became keeper of this little key, I dedicated myself to the task. I set aside for your petty expenditures the sum of one thousand francs a month. This, you will agree, is paid to you with the most scrupulous exactness. And you have the audacity to demand of me something additional for a mere whim — the gratification of an idle hour. Pray, what have you done to merit it ?

CHAMBLY *(pleading)*.— If you could only understand how the price of everything has gone up in Baden.

DELPHINE.— Nonsense !

CHAMBLY *(pleadingly)*.— Petty expenditures particularly, more than great ones. A thousand francs a month don't begin to cover my expenses. And then, this is leap-year; that upsets all my accounts, you know.

DELPHINE.— No ; I am far too indulgent with you. Remember that horse I bought for you just before we left Paris — such a beauty !

CHAMBLY.— I remember, also, that every day while we were in Paris you had him harnessed to your coupé, and drove him in the Bois. Naturally, I was prevented from riding him — unless, indeed, I had equipped myself like the Postillion de Longjumeau, with big boots and a little whip, and had got astride of him before your carriage. No doubt I should have been admired ; but the novelty might have provoked criticism upon a civil engineer. So I preferred to be less striking, and to hire a horse from the riding school.

DELPHINE.— Yes ; you confess it. Your money is wasted in hippodromes, in theatres, in fencing. You know you are a pillar of the fencing club.

CHAMBLY.— One moment, Madame Chambly. Do you remember what you said to me the year before our marriage ?

DELPHINE *(laughing)*.— That's too much to ask me, considering all I have said since.

CHAMBLY.— At that time I had just made your acquaintance. You were in mourning for my respected predecessor. The tears were hardly dry in your charming eyes. I urged my suit with ardor. It was at Auteuil, and your old dragon of an aunt was dozing over her after-dinner coffee. You heard my declaration, and laughed in my face.

DELPHINE.— That was very wrong of me,— to laugh, I mean,— considering my recent bereavement! *(Laughs.)* Ha! ha! ha!

CHAMBLY.— To me there was nothing funny about it. "Why can you not love me?" I asked mournfully. "Because I have vowed never to marry again," you answered. "But there must be some other reason," I urged. "Well, then, my dear M. Chambly, you are — if you will have it — you are —" "Go on; put me out of my misery, madame." "You are *too fat!*" The fact is I was immense — nothing poetical about me. "I will grow thin or die!" I exclaimed. From that moment I went in for athletics. I lifted heavy weights; I struggled daily with hundreds of pounds of solid metal, saying to myself the while, "It is for her. Great Heaven,— for her I love!" I flew to Griset; I took up fencing; five hours a day of thrust, of tierce, of riposte, of flanconnade — the fire of love directing me, every energy bent upon the overthrow of my adversary; ten — twelve foils were broken in my resistless fury of attack. I suffered dreadfully from lumbago; but I became poetical — I grew thin.

DELPHINE *(laughing)*.— And this was all for me? *(Rises and crosses, R. to table, leaves parasol there.)*

CHAMBLY.— And you never even noticed it? *(Changes tone.)* See here, Delphine, you have n't so much as a miserable little rag of a thousand-franc note in your pocketbook? I want an advance on next month. I am obliged to have a little money in hand. Have you forgotten that to-morrow is the birthday of the Grand Duke?

DELPHINE *(turns toward mirror)*.— Do you propose making a present to the Grand Duke?

CHAMBLY.— H-h-ardly, since he has not the privilege of my acquaintance.

DELPHINE *(leans on chair, menacing him with her fore-finger).*—You want money to play with!! Deny it, if you can. And you—shall—not—have—a—single *sou*, monsieur; mark that!!! *(She goes up, to mirror.)*

CHAMBLY *(aside).*—And I have but three miserable florins in my pocket! Jove, but a man is verdant in his honey-moon!

DELPHINE *(over her shoulder).*—Try to overcome this absurd passion. Go and take a walk; visit the environs of the town; admire the beauties of nature, the landscape.

CHAMBLY *(aside).*—Landscape! The only landscape I care for is a green table. Bah! with three florins in hand, a man *may* break the bank!

(Enter Jean, running.)

JEAN.—Monsieur called for me?

CHAMBLY.—No.

JEAN.—Beg pardon, monsieur and madame; but do monsieur and madame dine at the hotel to-day?

DELPHINE *(over her right shoulder).*—I don't know. Stay, was it not you who carried up our trunks yesterday?

JEAN *(bows).*—Yes, madame.

DELPHINE.—I forgot to pay you. Monsieur Chambly, will you give this boy three florins for his trouble?

CHAMBLY *(thunderstruck).*—Three florins!

DELPHINE *(laughs).*—You can't accommodate me with so small a sum?

CHAMBLY.—Of course! *(To Jean.)* Here it is.

DELPHINE *(sharply).*—Then why should you have hesitated?

CHAMBLY.—One is never quick enough for you, my dear.

DELPHINE *(pettishly, walking away to mantel-piece).*—Don't talk to me.

CHAMBLY.—Pray, my dear——

DELPHINE.—Bah!

JEAN *(aside).*—She was a widow when he married her, I'll take my oath to it, or she'd never be so uppish!

CHAMBLY *(aside to Jean).*—Halloa, you fellow! Give me back my three florins.

JEAN.— But, monsieur ——

CHAMBLY *(mysteriously).*—Hush! It is counterfeit money! If it is found upon you, you are lost.

JEAN *(terrified).*—Here it is, monsieur.

CHAMBLY *(aside).*—Now, if the double zero stands my friend.

DELPHINE *(arranging her bonnet, at mirror).*—Monsieur Chambly, are you coming?

CHAMBLY.— Ready, my dear. At your service always!

> *(They go out.)*

JEAN.— The gentleman is not so much his own master as when I saw him last. I *knew* I was not mistaken. He's the same party I served breakfast to when I was at the Café Anglais in Paris ——

> *(Enter Albert and Clotilde, arm in arm.)*

CLOTILDE.— Oh, what a lovely walk!

JEAN *(aside).*— The turtle doves in No. 4. *(Aloud.)* Beg pardon, monsieur and madame; but will monsieur and madame take dinner at the hotel?

ALBERT.— No. What do you say, darling, to an excursion? Suppose we visit the Château de la Favorite, and dine — no matter where!

CLOTILDE *(sentimentally).*— Oh, yes; anywhere! Under an arbor; far from everything!

JEAN *(aside).*— In their honeymoon, and no mistake. Makes me think about getting married myself! *(Exit.)*

CLOTILDE.—Was there ever such a lovely place as Baden?

ALBERT.—Never — except the spot where we were wed!

CLOTILDE.— Everybody seems so happy here. I see nothing but smiles and pretty toilettes. And then I love the music. How gay the shops are! Did you notice that jeweler's we passed coming back?

ALBERT.— What — Mellerio's ?

CLOTILDE.— Yes, darling. He had in his window such a pair of diamond ear-rings! *(Sighs.)* They were perfect ducks! Did n't you notice them ?

ALBERT.— No, I was looking at the cigars, next door.

CLOTILDE.— They were set in silver!

ALBERT.— What, the cigars ?

CLOTILDE.— Stupid boy. How they shone! Albert, if you wanted to be just too lovely for anything — I am wild about those ear-rings!

ALBERT.— Whom do you want most to please in all the world, Clotilde ?

CLOTILDE. — Why you, of course, dearest.

ALBERT.— The first time I saw you, darling, you were robed in simple white, wearing a flower in your belt.

CLOTILDE *(clings to his arm).* — Of course; I was just out of the convent.

ALBERT.— If you knew how enchanting I thought you then! Let me still feel that our love dates from yesterday. Let me see you ever as on that happy day. Need I give you those diamonds in order to bring a smile into your eyes ?

CLOTILDE.— No, but ——

ALBERT. — Then be satisfied now to be lovely and beloved, and one day, perhaps ——

CLOTILDE *(gayly).*— That is to say, you will give me the diamonds when you cease to love me — Then I would rather *never* have them !

ALBERT.— You are an angel!

CLOTILDE.— Never mind the ear-rings! I am going off to dress now, and you will see what gown I shall choose.

ALBERT. — Coquette !

CLOTILDE.— A little white frock, a blue sash, and a single flower worn in the belt. Will that please monsieur ? *(Albert puts his arm around her and kisses her brow.)* If any-one should see us what *would* they say ?

ALBERT.— That I love you.

CLOTILDE.— Then kiss me once more, but be quick about it.

(Chambly enters, R. He perceives couple, and coughs.)

CLOTILDE *(shrinking).*— How perfectly dreadful! We are seen. *(She runs off, L.)*

ALBERT *(recognizing Chambly).*— Prosper Chambly! My old comrade at St. Barbe!

CHAMBLY.— Albert de Rieux! Who would have thought of meeting you here. Why, my dear fellow, when last we parted, a dozen years ago, you had a Latin essay in your pocket. Now, when I meet you again, you've a pretty woman in your arms. Ha! ha!

ALBERT *(with dignity).* — I shall have pleasure in presenting you to my wife.

CHAMBLY.— You are married! So am I. What a coincidence.

ALBERT.— The most charming young girl——

CHAMBLY.— Mine's a magnificent widow!

ALBERT.— A widow?

CHAMBLY.— A widow. That has always been my dream. A young girl knows nothing of life, of character. Her experiments may so easily make shipwreck of your happiness. A widow, now—there are no whims, no illusions about *her!* If she has been unhappy with her *first,* she is the more disposed to be satisfied with number two. Or if she has been devoted to number one, she is inspired by tenderness to make the most of number two. Why do you laugh? This is sound logic, let me tell you, man. Now for yourself. Since when are you a Benedict?

ALBERT.— We were married six weeks ago. A love match, as you may believe.

CHAMBLY *(eagerly).*— Albert, do you keep the key of the secretary, or does she?

ALBERT.— The key of the common fund, do you mean —

the purse-strings, in other words ?   Why, I do, of course.
Why should you ask ?

CHAMBLY.— Oh, nothing !   Of course you do ; every man
does — I do, too.   The husband must rule, of course.
(Aside.)   What a lucky devil he is !

ALBERT.— And you and your wife have come to visit
Baden just as we have.   For health and pleasure, hey ?

CHAMBLY.— Yes ; we find it charming.   The Black Forest,
the old Château, the climate, not to speak of the balls and
concerts, and — ah ! — ahem — the roulette table.

ALBERT.— You 've tried your luck, then ?

CHAMBLY *(shrugs).*— Oh, nothing to speak of.   A mere
pastime.   Now and then, from time to time, merely to
amuse myself, I slip a few florins upon the double zero —
behind the scenes, you know.

ALBERT.— I see.   Madame does n't approve of it !   By the
way, Chambly, was it not you I saw last night, in the
company of two young officers, put a few gold pieces upon
the double zero ?

CHAMBLY *(reluctantly).*— Y-e-s, it was I.   Strange to
say, I lost, which seemed to afford some amusement to those
confounded youngsters.   But, as they laughed in German,
I did n't mind.

ALBERT.— I unfortunately understood their taunts; and
seeing in you a compatriot, I took it on me to resent their
ill-timed pleasantry.

CHAMBLY.— You became involved in a quarrel on my
account !   Generous as of old, and as ready as ever you
were to set lance in rest for the oppressed.   Let me recom-
mend you to be more careful, my good fellow ——

ALBERT *(carelessly).*— After giving them my plain
opinion of their impertinence, I put myself at the disposi-
tion of these warriors, and still await them.

CHAMBLY *(cautiously, looking about him).*— My dear fellow,
are you not very impetuous ?

ALBERT.— What! This from a swordsman so renowned as you, Monsieur Chambly?

CHAMBLY.—Yes; but I took up the art of war as a mere hygienic exercise. I wanted to lose flesh. For my part, I hold dueling in horror. But I am none the less obliged to you, my gallant comrade. *(Enter Delphine, R.)*

DELPHINE. — Monsieur Chambly.

CHAMBLY.—My dear, you will allow me to present to you Monsieur le Vicomte de Rieux, the Pythias to my Damon in schoolboy days.

ALBERT.— Who dares claim a corner by the fireside of your friendship, Madame Chambly.

DELPHINE *(curtsies).*—Monsieur, it is yours already. Have I not often heard my dear Prosper talk about your early intercourse at St. Barbe? *(Enter Clotilde, L.)*

CLOTILDE.— I 'm ready, Albert — Oh!

DELPHINE *(runs to meet her).*— Clotilde!

CLOTILDE *(embracing her fervently).*— Delphine!

CHAMBLY *(astonished).*— Our wives know each other! How very odd. This is the kind of thing they 'd put into a comedy, and the newspapers would say it was n't true to life.

DELPHINE *(her arm around Clotilde's waist).*— I should think we do know each other; were n't we together in the convent? So you, monsieur, are the husband of my dear little Clotilde?

CHAMBLY *(to Albert).*— De Rieux, we had better leave these ladies for a while. They must have an extraordinary amount to say.

DELPHINE.— We shall find enough to say about you both, don't fear!

CHAMBLY.— Good or evil?

CLOTILDE.— Just what you deserve!

CHAMBLY.— Let us be off, Albert, leaving our reputations in their hands. *(Aside.)* I am dying to try the luck of my last three florins upon the double zero. O honeymoon, how deceitfully you shine on all alike! Come on, De Rieux, come on. *(Exeunt Chambly and Albert, C.)*

DELPHINE.— Now come, Clotilde, tell me all about your marriage.

CLOTILDE.— It's your turn first, Delphine. You have had so much more experience. You left the convent three years before me, recollect.

DELPHINE.— True. How awfully old I am! Well, my dear little Clotilde, hardly had I quitted the convent, where we were so gay, so joyous, when I married Monsieur——

CLOTILDE *(joyfully)*.— Yes, you married Albert's friend. How nice! It's just what I should have liked to do if I had n't married Albert.

DELPHINE.— Oh, no! Did I not mention it? When I married Monsieur Chambly — *(very gayly)* — I was already a widow.

CLOTILDE *(laughs)*.— Two husbands in such a little while! But then you always were a clever creature.

DELPHINE.— Yes; I was the widow of M. de Varennes, who had made me as miserable as I could be. At first I thought nothing would induce me to take another husband. But M. Chambly was so kind, so persistent; I was so lonely, so young,— life with my old aunt at Auteuil was *so* dreary,— I accepted him!

CLOTILDE *(laughs)*.— You are very wise, my dear. As for my story, it is short. What can I tell but that I am Albert's wife!

DELPHINE.— The sum of earthly happiness!

CLOTILDE.— Is n't he too lovely, Delphine? But *(gazing at Delphine fixedly)* ——

DELPHINE.—Very much so. Handsome and distinguished. But what are you looking at?

CLOTILDE *(in a pathetic tone)*.— Your diamond ear-rings.

DELPHINE *(carelessly)*.— Pretty, are n't they ? We bought them yesterday at Mellerio's.

CLOTILDE *(sighs)*.— Ah !

DELPHINE.— What is the matter, child ? If you fancy them, there is a pair left exactly like these.

CLOTILDE *(sadly)*.— I know it.

DELPHINE.— Ask your husband to buy them for you.

CLOTILDE *(with pathos)*.— I have already done so.

DELPHINE.— Well ?

CLOTILDE *(sighs)*.— No matter, let us talk of other things.

DELPHINE *(gayly)*.— No, let us talk of diamond ear-rings.

CLOTILDE *(reluctantly)*.— Well, Albert gave me to understand that ——

DELPHINE.— He refused you ?

CLOTILDE *(sighing)*.— Ye-e-s.

DELPHINE *(tragically)*.— Clotilde, you are *lost!*

CLOTILDE.— Lost ?

DELPHINE.— After only six weeks of marriage you allow your husband to say "No"? Clotilde, you are on the verge of a bottomless abyss!

CLOTILDE *(rising)*.— Delphine, you frighten me!

DELPHINE *(rising)*.— My poor, innocent child, don't you know your life's happiness depends on the stand you take during the honeymoon ? Oh, it was your lucky star that led you to my hands. If you want those diamonds, you *must* have them — there !

CLOTILDE.—But when I tell you that Albert has declined to give them to me — that I have already begged for them ——

DELPHINE *(eagerly)*.— In a melting voice, with a tender look, whilst you hung upon his arm ?

CLOTILDE.— Yes; the very best I could.

DELPHINE.— Don't be too sure. In the arsenal of feminine coquetry there is a certain glance, accompanied by a certain attitude — See, this way — Fold your hands and drop your voice to an appealing whisper — " Albert, my Albert! you can refuse *me* what I ask ? "

CLOTILDE *(doubtfully).*— I *think* I might do that.

DELPHINE.—Try.

CLOTILDE *(stiffly, imitating).*— "Albert, my Albert! you can refuse me what I ask ? "

DELPHINE *(discouraged).*— No, that is not a success. Try again.

CLOTILDE.— Oh, how discouraging! I can't pretend. Is there no other way ?

DELPHINE.— I 'm thinking. Ah, I have it ! Can you cry ?

CLOTILDE *(curiously).* — Cry ?

DELPHINE *(spells).*— Yes ; C - R -Y, you know! Why, of course you do. All women know how to cry. Between ourselves, my dear, men are less black than we paint them. When we weep, they can't resist us.

CLOTILDE *(gayly).*— I never thought of that.

DELPHINE.— It is almost sure to succeed. My poor first husband, whose temper was bad enough, dear knows, was invariably softened by my tears. Try it with M. de Rieux, and you will be astonished at the result.

CLOTILDE.— My good Delphine !

DELPHINE.— Oh, the eloquence of tears is infallible. You shall see !

CLOTILDE.— But how does one cry when there is nothing to cry about ?

DELPHINE.— Make believe ; put your handkerchief to your eyes, sob, work yourself up to the idea that you are a martyr, and the tears will come of themselves.

(Enter Albert, C.)

Ah! your husband !

ALBERT.— Are the confidences over ?

DELPHINE.— Yes ; and I give back your little Clotilde, the wiser for my experience. *(To Clotilde, aside.)* I shall

leave you to practice on him. Be brave, and all will go well.
(Aloud to Albert.)   And what have you done with my husband, M. de Rieux ?   Did you lose him by the way ?

ALBERT.— No ; he — ahem — is listening to the band.

DELPHINE.— The band ?   Since when has he become a
connoisseur of music ?   Well, I shall try to bring back my
wanderer.   Au revoir, my friends ; we shall soon meet
again.   *(Exit Delphine, R.)*

ALBERT.— What a charming, spirited wife Chambly has !

CLOTILDE.— Yes ; we all loved her at the convent.

ALBERT.— Chambly is a capital fellow.   He would make
any woman happy.

CLOTILDE *(pathetically)*.— Delphine is happy.   He refuses
her nothing.   Only yesterday he gave her ——

ALBERT.— Well, what ?

CLOTILDE *(sighs)*.— The very diamonds you refused to
give me.   And they have been two years married !

ALBERT *(annoyed)*.— Ah !

CLOTILDE *(hesitating)*.— If you only knew how I have set
my heart on them.   *(Aside.)*   I have n't really, but Delphine
says my future is at stake !

ALBERT.— Diamonds are cold, ugly stones, not at all
suited to your fresh young beauty.

CLOTILDE.— It *may* be a caprice ; but, oh ! I can think of
nothing else.

ALBERT *(smiling)*.— Then don't you think it is my duty to
wean you from caprice ?   Come, try to forget them, for my
sake.

CLOTILDE *(voice trembling)*.— I did n't think such a little
sum as two or three thousand francs would stand between
us, Albert.

ALBERT *(aside)*.— How prettily she pleads !   Confound
the money, I don't care for that ; but, if I give up now, I 'm
gone.

CLOTILDE *(aside)*.— That *was* a hit !   Let me try again.

(Aloud.) Albert, my Albert! you can refuse *me* what I ask?

ALBERT *(movement toward her).*—Clotilde! my darling! *(Aside.)* If I don't stand firm, all 's up!

CLOTILDE *(aside).*—I am certainly improving. *(Aloud.)* Here is your hat, dearest; we will go together to the jeweler's.

ALBERT.—I will give you anything in the world, Clotilde, except those diamonds. Come, be reasonable, and yield the point.

CLOTILDE *(aside).*—There is one thing left. Delphine says my happiness depends on it. *(Bursts into tears.)* Ah! Albert, I am so unhappy!

ALBERT *(astonished).*—Clotilde!

CLOTILDE *(sobbing).*—Six weeks of marriage, and it has come to this!

ALBERT.—But, Clotilde ——

CLOTILDE.—You don't love me. You have never loved me!

ALBERT *(aside).*—Hang it, I can't stand tears.

CLOTILDE.—My poor mother! She alone loves me, in all this weary world!

ALBERT.—Clotilde, dearest, and I have made you cry? Oh, what a brute I am!

CLOTILDE.—Leave me! All is over!

ALBERT *(on his knees beside her).*—Be calm, darling. I will fly at once and fetch those miserable diamonds.

CLOTILDE.—Oh! no, no, no! I shall never want *anything* again.

ALBERT.—In a few moments they shall be laid at your feet.

CLOTILDE *(hiding her face).*—I am going back to the convent!

ALBERT.—Clotilde, don't say such cruel words. There, kiss me. I 'm off to fetch those ear-rings.

(Exit Albert impetuously, L.)

CLOTILDE (*drying her eyes*).— *Real* tears! What a success! Delphine was right. I had no idea of it.

(*Chambly comes in with an abstracted air, C.*)

CHAMBLY.—The double zero refused to come up. Queer, is n't it ?

CLOTILDE.—M. Chambly!

CHAMBLY (*not observing her*).—If it were near the first of the month! Here it is only the 24th, and I have n't another franc at my command. This month has thirty-one days, and these are the longest days of the whole year. Let me see ——   (*Enter Jean, R.*)

JEAN (*suddenly*).— Monsieur called me ?

CHAMBLY (*angrily*).—No ; get out with you !

JEAN.—I thought monsieur called me, on account of the little trifle of twenty francs that monsieur owes me ——

CHAMBLY.— Get out, you rascal !

JEAN.—Certainly, sir ; going this minute. I have entire confidence in monsieur's honesty ——

CHAMBLY (*aside*).— Go to the devil with your confidence. (*Exit Jean. Clotilde comes forward as Albert runs in, R.*)

ALBERT (*box in hand*).—Clotilde ! I have come to sue for pardon.

CLOTILDE (*aside, triumphantly*).— He has them !

CHAMBLY (*aside, surprised*). — For pardon ?

CLOTILDE (*aside*).— Poor Albert ! to have deceived him thus ! I dare not accept those ear-rings.

ALBERT.— You are still vexed with me ? If you knew the trouble I had to get them !

CLOTILDE.— How ?

ALBERT.— A gentleman was in the very act of buying them. The fact is, these diamonds are beauties. I don't know how I could have resisted them before. I bid over him, and the prize was mine. (*Shows case with jewels.*) See here, Chambly, how they sparkle !

CHAMBLY. — Yes ; they are exactly like my wife's.

ALBERT.—Like those you gave your wife, you mean ?

CHAMBLY.— Not at all. Like those my wife obligingly bestowed upon herself a day or two since.

CLOTILDE *(confused, taking the case of jewels).*— Albert — M. Chambly — if you will excuse me, I will go to my room and try the effect of my new ornaments.

ALBERT.— All right, dear. I will finish my letter, and be with you in a moment. *(He sits down at desk, L.)*

CLOTILDE *(aside, going out).*— All the same, one pays dearly for a lie ! *(Exit Clotilde, L.)*

CHAMBLY *(aside).*— He 's in funds, evidently ! I sha'n't hesitate to borrow enough to set me on my feet again. *(To Albert.)* My dear fellow !

ALBERT *(without looking up).*— You 're off ?

CHAMBLY.— Yes ; but I say, old fellow, here 's a bore !

ALBERT *(still writing).* — What 's up ?

CHAMBLY *(feeling in his pockets).*— I stupidly forgot to put any money in my pocket. Have you by chance five louis about you ?

ALBERT *(giving him gold).*— Entirely at your service.

CHAMBLY. — Thanks, I 'll return it to you this evening.

ALBERT *(carelessly).* — Suit your own convenience.

CHAMBLY *(aside).* — Then I 'll pay on the second of next month. *(Aloud.)* You are going out ?

ALBERT *(seals his letter).*— Only to drop this letter in the box, when I shall be at the command of my wife.

CHAMBLY.— O ye turtle-doves !

ALBERT. — But she 's such a little angel, Chambly. You 've really no idea what an angel she is !

(Exit Albert, C. Enter Jean, R.)

JEAN *(suddenly).* — Monsieur called me ?

CHAMBLY *(buttoning up his coat over the gold).*— No, get out with you.

JEAN.— It 's no matter, monsieur. Monsieur knows I have every confidence in monsieur's honesty.

CHAMBLY *(laughing)*. — Here, you impudent rascal; here are your twenty francs. Let's hear no more from you.

JEAN. — I suppose *this* is good money, Monsieur Chambly? Ha! ha! ha!

CHAMBLY. — As I look at you, you grinning idiot, I seem to recognize that stupid face. Where have I seen it before?

JEAN. — I once had the honor to serve monsieur's breakfast at the Café Anglais, in Paris. I thought we recognized each other, monsieur. But I was thrown off the track by the fact of monsieur's being now a married man.

CHAMBLY. — Unfortunately, I omitted to send you wedding cards. But I had not your address, you know. You'll excuse me?

JEAN. — Oh, certainly, monsieur.

CHAMBLY. — You are very kind. *(Aside.)* Just the same idiot he always was. The borders of the Rhine have n't changed him in the least. Well, I'm off. With four louis, and good luck, I can — *(Aloud.)* If Madame Chambly asks for me, you will say that I have gone to admire the beauties of nature. Ah, there she comes.

(Exit Chambly, L. Enter Delphine, R.)

DELPHINE. — Monsieur Chambly is not here?

JEAN *(bows)*. — No, madame, he is not here — he never was here — that is, he bid me say to madame that he has gone to admire the beauties of nature.

(Exit Jean, confused, R. Enter Clotilde, dressed in white, with jewels in her ears, L.)

DELPHINE. — Clotilde, let me kiss you! How did it work?

CLOTILDE *(joyously, showing her diamonds)*. — Judge for yourself!   *(Albert appears at door.)*

DELPHINE. — You must have cried *very* hard.

CLOTILDE *(dropping her eyes)*. — The best I could, dear.

DELPHINE *(laughs)*. — I can imagine the scene! He was

so remorseful, so repentant! Ha! ha! ha! It's a snare as old as love! No man can escape it. Poor, dear Albert. Ha! ha! ha!

CLOTILDE.— I had some compunction — *(archly)* — not much.

DELPHINE.— Not much -- ha! ha! No. I fancy not. What a child you still are, Clotilde. And now, my dear, to celebrate our victory, these husbands of ours shall take us to dinner at the restaurant. Fetch your gloves and parasol. All Baden shall do homage to your diamonds. Come quickly ——
(They go out laughing, R.
Albert comes forward as
Chambly enters, L.)

ALBERT.— And I am the dupe of these designing women! Oh, it is contemptible!

CHAMBLY *(absorbed in his own thoughts)*.—Yes; it is really contemptible.

ALBERT *(surprised)*.— What do you mean?

CHAMBLY.— That confounded double zero! This time it came up.

ALBERT.— Well, and what of that?

CHAMBLY.—You don't understand. This time I had changed the combination. I put my stakes on thirty-six.

ALBERT *(absorbed in himself)*.— And I was fool enough to be really cut up. *(Goes up, R.)*

CHAMBLY.— What do you think I am? I have n't a solitary franc left. Hallo! Where are you off to?

ALBERT *(going)*.—I have a headache — heart-ache. I must get a little air.

CHAMBLY.— You 've been losing, too?

ALBERT.— Nothing to speak of — only my little all.

CHAMBLY.—You are joking, Albert. On what number?

ALBERT *(bitterly)*.— I have lost faith forever in my wife.

CHAMBLY.—Faith — is that all? Bah! Faith is easily renewed. It springs up like an aftermath.

ALBERT. —Suppose I were to tell you that your wife —
my wife — both our wives — are — monsters of duplicity ;
that they are leagued together to destroy our happiness?

CHAMBLY. — Nonsense.

ALBERT. — That together they revel in hypocrisy, coin
sentiments to betray us with, invent soft speeches to ruin
us ; feign tears, and after they have wrung from us what
they want ——

CHAMBLY *(sadly)*. — Not Delphine, I 'm sure. She 's no
need for that.

ALBERT. — She, if anything, is the worse. *She* leads the
way, and my wife follows. *She* is the high priest, Clotilde
the neophyte. " Weep, weep, my dear," counsels your
insidious wife, "and *nothing* will be refused to you."

CHAMBLY. — What 's that ?

ALBERT. — Oh, I can't stand the thought of it — I 'm
off —— *(Exit Albert, C.)*

CHAMBLY. — What did he say ? Delphine said, " Weep,
weep, and nothing will be refused to you!" An idea
comes to me. A light breaks on my darkened pathway.
Let me see. History tells us that Monaldeschi, reader to
Queen Christine, wept systematically and successfully when-
ever he wanted anything from the queen. I really don't
see why the lachrymose method should not succeed as
well in the Grand Duchy of Baden as it did in the King-
dom of Sweden. Here she comes.

*(He looks out of window, C.
Delphine enters, R., in walking dress.)*

DELPHINE *(gaily)*. — Well, Monsieur Chambly, you seem
preoccupied.

CHAMBLY *(sighs)*. —I was wrapt in contemplation of the
beauties of nature, my dear. A view like this is balm to
the wounded spirit. *(Aside.)* Not bad for a beginner.

DELPHINE *(surprised)*. — Ah !

CHAMBLY *(looking through window)*.—How sweetly pensive is the light of the setting sun, as it slants athwart yon antique mill — and the donkey in the foreground!

DELPHINE *(looks at him)*.— And the donkey in the foreground! I quite agree with you.

CHAMBLY *(aside)*.— I'm afraid the melancholy won't work as well as I had hoped.

DELPHINE *(with animation)*.— Do you know, my love, that we are to dine to-day at the restaurant? A jolly party of four — with Monsieur and Madame de Rieux!

CHAMBLY.— Delightful, my love — and — ah — I've just got a letter from my tailor. The stupid fellow has the assurance to ask me for five hundred francs by the next mail.

DELPHINE.— How odd! Your tailor has written to you here — at Baden?

CHAMBLY *(uneasily)*.—Deucedly impudent, was n't it? It's always impudent when a tailor wants his money, is n't it?

DELPHINE *(calmly)*.— Show me his letter.

CHAMBLY.— The strangest thing! I lit my cigar with it.

DELPHINE.— But you don't smoke.

CHAMBLY.—That's true! I don't smoke —certainly, I don't smoke. But coming out from play just now I met a man,— he was coming out from play just now, I mean,— and he was smoking -- he wanted to smoke, I mean — and I lit *his* cigarette; exactly — that was the way of it.

DELPHINE.— You said, first, that your tailor's letter was used to light a cigar.

CHAMBLY.— Ette — ette. In my hurry I dropped the end of it, that 's all. I *meant* a cigarette.

DELPHINE.— Very clear, indeed! And so this gentleman could n't light his own cigarette?

CHAMBLY *(desperately)*.— Did n't I tell you? He was an old soldier — a veteran in the last war, poor fellow, who had both arms shot off by a cannon-ball.

(Enter Jean, C., arranges chair, etc.)

DELPHINE *(satirically).*— You are not strong in invention, my dear. I would advise you to cultivate your imagination before the next time you are in need of funds.

CHAMBLY *(appealingly).*— Delphine!

DELPHINE *(deliberately).*— And, as I see plainly that your passion for play is on the increase, you shall not have another franc from me.

CHAMBLY.— As you please! Oh, what a miserable life is mine! *(He falls into a chair and bursts into tears.)*

DELPHINE.— Eh! What is this?

CHAMBLY *(weeping).*— Oh! I see it all now. My life has been a sacrifice — I am no longer beloved!

DELPHINE.— What's the matter with him now?

CHAMBLY.— Nobody loves me. Oh, my mother — my poor, poor mother! Why did I ever leave her?

> *(At back, Jean takes out his hand-*
> *kerchief. Delphine bursts into*
> *hearty laughter.)*

DELPHINE.— If you only knew how ridiculous you look. Ha! ha! ha!

CHAMBLY.— Ridiculous!

> *(Jean bursts into audible sobs.)*

CHAMBLY *(sitting up).*— What is the matter with Jean?

DELPHINE.— Be comforted, you have touched one tender heart. Ha! ha! ha!

JEAN.— Beg pardon, monsieur, you look so pitiful. I can't stand it. *(He sobs.)*   *(Delphine laughs.)*

CHAMBLY *(aside).*— My sole success is with a hotel-waiter. This is humiliating!

JEAN *(approaches Chambly).*— Oh, monsieur, I'm not what they call rich — I have only sixty francs. Here they are *(sob)*; monsieur will give them back to me when he can *(sob).* I have every confidence in monsieur's honesty.

CHAMBLY *(waving him off).*— Leave me to myself, waiter. You cannot help me.

DELPHINE. — Here comes Clotilde. Perhaps that may induce you to stanch the flow of your tears.

CHAMBLY *(aside).* — So it appears, I'm an utter failure. The truth is, I have never learned to cry. I wonder if I could take lessons somewhere. *(Enter Clotilde, L., with hat on, parasol, etc.)*

CLOTILDE. — I'm sorry to have kept you waiting. Well, are we ready to set out?

DELPHINE. — We are ready, I believe.

CLOTILDE *(looking about her).* — My husband is n't here?

JEAN *(looks out of window).* — If I may take the liberty to speak, monsieur is at this moment walking up and down like mad, in the poplar alley, yonder.

CLOTILDE. — We will pick him up, on the way. Why, what is the matter with Monsieur Chambly?

JEAN *(interposing).* — Take no notice, madame. By the way, madame, I have just remembered that the proprietor charged me to give a letter to madame. I have it somewhere — Ah! here it is. *(Produces letter, hands it to Clotilde.)*

CLOTILDE. — A letter from the proprietor! I wonder why he sent it to me instead of to my husband.

JEAN *(indifferently).* — I can't say, madame, really. But it is probably important, because the proprietor observed that it concerns the life of Monsieur de Rieux, which is in immediate danger.

DELPHINE. — Danger — his life!

CLOTILDE *(screams).* — Albert! Heavens! if he should be lost!

CHAMBLY *(dreamily).* — Lost! Yes, on that double zero.

DELPHINE *(takes letter from Clotilde).* — Let me see, dear. *(reads)* "Madame: Yesterday, at the gaming table, your husband took sides against three young officers who were amusing themselves at the expense of one of his compatriots."

CHAMBLY *(listening)*. — That was I !

DELPHINE *(reads)*. — " Although in the wrong, these officers could not brook the defiant rebuke of Monsieur le
Vicomte de Rieux, and they have publicly announced
that they will demand satisfaction at his hands, upon his
appearance in the gaming hall to-day. As a well-wisher,
let me counsel you to restrain Monsieur le Vicomte from
setting foot in the place mentioned ; for should he do so,
he is lost ! "

CHAMBLY. — Sapristi !

DELPHINE. — Well, monsieur, so you intend to remain
here ? You, who are the source of all this trouble ?

CHAMBLY *(calmly)*.— Oh, never fear. I myself will under-
take to settle the whole affair in the most amicable style.

CLOTILDE *(clasping her hands)*. — Only do so, my good,
kind friend, and I will love you always.

DELPHINE *(to Chambly)*.—Hurry, Chambly. You might
have been there by this time.

CHAMBLY.—Never fear ! Never fear ! *(Aside.)* And
what the devil am I in for, now ? Sapristi !

(Exit, C., followed by Jean.)

CLOTILDE *(distracted)*. —Delphine, while your husband
has gone to intercept those cruel, bloodthirsty officers, I
shall fly to Albert, cling to his dear neck, and implore him,
for my sake, not to fight.

DELPHINE.—Not at all. The sensible thing to do
will be to hide the whole affair from him. Don't let him
leave your side to-day, or allow him to go near those
horrid gaming-rooms. To-morrow morning, by dawn of
day, you must find some pretext for setting out for Paris.
(Returns letter.)

CLOTILDE.— Right, Delphine. You were always so wise
and calm. Thank Heaven ! here he comes.

(Enter Albert, C.)

ALBERT.— And why are you in such confusion, may
I ask ?

DELPHINE *(aside to Clotilde).*—He knows nothing. Only keep him at your side.

ALBERT *(coldly, to both ladies).*—Are you about to take a walk before dinner ?

CLOTILDE *(takes off her hat and sits on sofa).*—No ; I don't care to walk, thanks.

ALBERT *(shrugs).*—As you will. Chambly has gone out ?

DELPHINE *(sits on other end of sofa from Clotilde).*—Chambly wants to see you particularly. He will be back directly. Sit down, M. de Rieux — here, between us. That is as it should be.

ALBERT *(stiffly, sits).*—You are very kind.

DELPHINE *(takes out embroidery).*—Just before you came in, Clotilde and I were having a good, old-fashioned chat — a woman's gossip about gowns and novels.

ALBERT *(with emphasis).*—Emotional, no doubt !

DELPHINE.—Clotilde prefers — *(aside to Clotilde)* Brace up, my dear — *(aloud)* Balzac.

CLOTILDE *(with effort).*—And Delphine prefers George Sand. What is your idea, Monsieur de Rieux ?

ALBERT *(looking from one to the other).*—In my opinion, all novels are alike. There is the inevitable heroine, plunged into the inevitable love-scrape, who sheds the inevitable tears. Of all things, I despise tears ! Then there is the inevitable fool of a lover, who allows himself to be imposed on by those tears. Am I not right, Clotilde ?

DELPHINE.—My dear Monsieur de Rieux, you have suddenly grown cynical. In a little while you will grow dull. Am I not right, Clotilde ?

ALBERT *(coldly).*—Clotilde will not dispute *you*, Madame Chambly. *(Looks at watch.)* An hour yet before dinner. *(Rises.)*

CLOTILDE *(impetuously, hand on Albert's arm).*—Oh, don't go out, Albert !

ALBERT.—Why ? if I may ask !

DELPHINE *(points to window).*— Look at that great cloud gathering. We shall have a fearful storm.

ALBERT.— All the better. Nothing is so grand as a storm in these mountains. Chambly and I will enjoy it together.

(Turns, up stage.)

CLOTILDE *(tearfully).*— Albert!

ALBERT *(turns, coldly).*— You did me the honor to speak, madame?

CLOTILDE.— Albert, I beseech you, I *entreat* you, to stay here — close to my side.

ALBERT.— You surprise me. I can't understand how I can add to your knowledge of gowns and novels. If you wish my experience in woman's tears — now — *(Offers to go.)*

CLOTILDE *(springing toward him).*— Albert, you are cruel. If you love me, stay!

DELPHINE.— Monsieur de Rieux, do you not see the poor child is suffering?

(Clotilde bursts into tears.)

ALBERT.— *Tears* again, Madame de Rieux! Are you already in the mood to change your diamonds?

CLOTILDE *(extending her hand).* —Have mercy!

ALBERT *(to Delphine).* —Your scholar makes rapid progress, does she not, madame? By ill-luck, a short time since, you ladies undertook to chant the psalm of victory, aloud — and, by ill-luck, I overheard you ——

CLOTILDE *(despairingly).*—He will never believe in me again!

ALBERT *(coldly).* —You are right. Too well you knew my blind confidence in you; you knew that every one of your tears would find its way to my heart. Counting upon this, you had recourse to simulated grief, and afterward — you laughed at me! What mattered it to you? — the comedy had succeeded. There I was, on my knees at your side, imploring your pardon, and offering you those miserable gewgaws. What did you care that I was made sport of? You had your diamonds; you could afford to laugh at me.

CLOTILDE.— Albert, have mercy! It was all a jest!

ALBERT *(paying no attention).* — Yours was an easy triumph. But now that my eyes are opened, these tears, summoned at will, make no impression. No; I believe in you no longer. Sorrow and tears, common enough in the lot of most of us, should be held sacred from idle jesting. You have not only wounded me, Clotilde, you have deceived me. Farewell!

CLOTILDE *(with a strong effort, passing from tears to laughter).* —No, no, Albert. You won't leave me thus. I cannot bear it. See, I'm not crying now. You are right. Tears are deceitful things. But you'll believe me when I *smile?* Why, I am laughing — don't you see?

> *(She changes again from laughter to tears, and falls sobbing on the sofa. Albert looks in astonishment at Delphine, who snatches the letter from Clotilde's gown, and hands it to him.)*

DELPHINE.— Read this, and you will understand.

CLOTILDE.— No, no; he must not. Give it to me.

DELPHINE.— Read it, Monsieur de Rieux.

> *(Albert tears open the letter, and reads the contents.)*

ALBERT. —Tears! *Real* tears, and wrung from you by my danger! Clotilde, my darling! beloved by you, I shall live forever. Why, I *insist* upon living — now let me go! *(Enter Chambly, C., followed by Jean.)*

CHAMBLY.— It is too late.

ALBERT, DELPHINE, and CLOTILDE *(together).* —Chambly!

CHAMBLY *(gaily).* — Losing no time, I soon found our three adversaries — in line of battle, as it were — thirsting for our blood. I began by attempting to explain the affair; in my usual happy style, I endeavored to illustrate the pacific state of mind maintained by our side. Impossible to make them listen to reason. It's true they spoke German, while I spoke French.

ALBERT. — Go on; what happened?

CHAMBLY *(deliberately)*. — All in due time, my dear fellow. When I found that somebody must fight, I said to myself: " Well, you spent seven years in learning to break foils with old Griset, why not utilize your skill?" I wanted to assure myself that the old professor had earned his money fairly. At the same time, I reflected that it was on my account you got yourself into this scrape. To cut the matter short, I offered to fight all three of 'em!

DELPHINE *(draws near, with animation)*. — That was noble, Chambly!

CHAMBLY. — You flatter me, Delphine. Jean here, agreed to be my second, and together we set out for the field of blood. The combat was short and decisive. I wounded one of my adversaries, and the two others promptly accepted my friendly overtures.

ALBERT. — You actually wounded your man?

CHAMBLY. — A mere scratch — but it was enough to satisfy him. A charming young fellow, a most agreeable talker — in German, by the way.

JEAN *(enthusiastically)*. — Oh, monsieur fought like a lion.

CHAMBLY. — You are partial, Jean. To sum it all up, they have invited me to breakfast, this day week.

> *(Albert shakes hands with Chambly; the ladies salute him. Clotilde and Albert retire up, arm-in-arm.)*

DELPHINE. — Do you know what *I* think of all this, Monsieur Chambly?

CHAMBLY *(apologetically)*. — Be merciful with my infirmity, my dear! I 'll promise not to fight again this year.

DELPHINE. — On the contrary, I have never admired you so much as now. Ask of me what you will.

CHAMBLY.— Then in future, every time I am in want of money, must I kill a man to get it ?

DELPHINE.— No ; I mean to save you the exertion. You need fight no more duels. Here is a little token of my love.

(She extends to him the key of the
secretary. Chambly seizes her
hand and kisses it.)

CHAMBLY.— The key of the secretary ! Mine, once again ! Hurrah ! Now, tell me, you dear, forgiving creature, why is it that when women cry they get all they want from men,— while men get only laughter for their tears ?

DELPHINE *(laughs.)*— A woman *may*, possibly, look pretty when she cries, but a man — Oh ! if you could have seen yourself ! What an object !

CHAMBLY.— I suppose so, judging by Jean there. *(Points to Jean.)* He certainly was a fright ! And now, my friends, our dinner waits for us !

TABLEAU.

JEAN,
ALBERT, CLOTILDE,   CHAMBLY, DELPHINE.

Curtain.

BEHIND A CURTAIN

A MONOLOGUE

AS PLAYED BY MRS. CHARLES DENISON AT THE
MADISON SQUARE THEATRE
JAN. 14, 1887

BEHIND A CURTAIN, a Monologue, is given here, as played by Mrs. Denison (Miss Mathilde Madison), of the Madison Square Theatre, at the matinées of January 13th and 14th, 1887, and during the Summer of the same year, at the Rodick House, Bar Harbor. This Monologue has also been acted by Mrs. Walter Andrews and other amateurs in private houses. The scene represents a sitting-room in a hotel in New York. A curtained

bed may be used in one corner, or Mrs. Bellamy, in going to look for her burglar, may retire behind a screen, or go into an adjoining bedroom and return. It is perhaps needless to suggest that to hold an audience by a monologue requires constant action on the part of the player, and unflagging spirit. This one was rendered by Mrs. Denison with the addition of original "business," adding greatly to its success.

BEHIND A CURTAIN.

SCENE: *A room in a hotel in New York. Mrs. Bellamy, a young widow, dressed for traveling, bag in hand, comes in.*

MRS. BELLAMY *(speaking off)*.— There, that will do! See that my luggage is sent up? *(Comes forward.)* What a runaway! When I awoke this morning I had n't the least idea of sleeping in a strange hotel in New York. The truth is, I had to come. It was the only way to save myself from that tiresome Captain Fitzhenry. Worn out with trying to keep off a proposal, I finally consented to receive him at twelve this morning. At twelve this morning I was on the train —" called to New York on business of importance." Poor man! I should have liked to see his face when my butler gave the message. *(Laughs.)*

(Sits in chair.)— What a long journey from my country-house to town! I am tired to death! I wonder if Fitzhenry believed the butler! It 's true, I have an excuse for coming.

To-morrow is Augusta's wedding-day. Augusta was my dearest friend at school. When I was married before her, three years ago, she was quite green with jealousy; but when poor Mr. Bellamy died, six months after, leaving me all that money, Augusta was ready to tear my eyes out. Poor Augusta! she never could stand another person's luck!

(Knock at door.)

Well, who 's there? *(Goes to door, takes in letter.)* A letter! For me? Who possibly could know I am in town? Captain Fitzhenry's handwriting! Ridiculous!

(She tears open letter and reads.)

"Clever as you are, dear Mrs. Bellamy, you can't elude me. By judicious bribery of your servants, I managed to find out what train you took to town. I was, during the whole journey, in the rear car of your train. It was horribly dull there, in company with a maiden lady, who ate lozenges; but I was comforted by thinking, if an accident occurred, I should, at least, have the happiness of perishing with you. My cab followed yours to the hotel. To-morrow, at eleven, I shall present myself to receive my final answer.   Devotedly yours,

"FITZHENRY."

What incredible impertinence! I 'll refuse to see him. Have n't I said, over and over, that I will never marry again! What! sacrifice my life of enchanting independence for the sake of a man! Here I am, free to come and go as I please— *(Starts.)* What was that noise? How nervous one becomes in traveling alone! I wish my stupid maid had not sprained her ankle yesterday. Now I come to think of it, this is the first time I was ever at a hotel by myself. It certainly is not as pleasant as it looks. Suppose a burglar— I 'll look under the bed. *(Goes back, returns.)* No one there. I 'd better barricade the door. *(Piles up chairs.)* If any one comes in, I 'll hear it. I won't be murdered without knowing it. My death shall make a noise in the world, I promise you. *(Sits, takes up newspaper.)* It 's all the fault of these horrid newspapers. I never pick one up without reading some dreadful tale of robbery and murder. The villains seem to pick out solitary females; widows especially. *(Reads.)* "Only last week a young and charming widow — chloroformed at — her *hotel!*" Oh, if I had known that, I never would have come. *(Looks at curtain.)* Good gracious! what was that? Did n't the curtain move? What shall I do? Let me behave as if I noticed nothing. *(Takes up book on table, tries to read.)* What 's this — "Triumphant Burglary." *(Drops book, looks again at curtain.)* I see his feet! In great big boots, such as robbers always wear. Here I am, locked in with him. To reach the bell I 'd have to pass that window. I 'll die first. Horrible! To-morrow there 'll be a new murder to put in all the newspapers. A widow, alone, unfriended, in a strange hotel. How could he know I have my diamonds in this bag? What will Fitzhenry say when he comes here at eleven to-morrow, and finds me weltering in my gore? Poor Fitzhenry! he loves me. He would have saved me from this awful fate.

Oh, those feet, those feet. I dare not look at them again, and yet I must! Stay! If he is going to kill me for my diamonds, I 'll offer them to him. If he has a shadow of delicacy, he will accept them. *(Speaks to curtain, in a trembling voice.)* Sir, I know you are there, behind the curtain. You cannot hide from me, I have seen your feet. But do not be afraid, I won't summon the police. No doubt you are more unfortunate than guilty. A series of financial reverses may have impelled you to this method of earning a livelihood. Your wife, no doubt, is dying. Your children, poor little things, are gnawing crusts. I may seem to you angry and terrible, but indeed I 'm not. I am about to offer you my diamonds, every one, and all the money in my purse. Here they are *(shows jewel case)*, in this bag, most convenient for carrying in the hand. If you don't mind, I will keep one or two necessary things. My comb and brush, and my tooth-brush. They can be of no use to you. *(Takes out articles named, tears off bracelets and rings, puts them in bag, closes it, puts it on chair, pushes chair toward curtain.)* There, take it and go out by the window as you came. I'll shut my eyes, so as not to look at you. I couldn't identify you again, no matter how hard I might try. *(Shuts eyes, stands center stage, ears stopped. Pause. Opens eyes.)*

What! the bag still there? You won't take it? You persist in murdering me? *(Falls on knees.)* O Mr. Burglar, spare me! Have pity on a woman who never did you any harm!

(Knock at door.)

Who's there? Ah!

(Jumps up, rushes to door, upsets chair, opens it wildly.)

(Voice.) — Beg pardon, ma'am, but there's a pair o' boots in there, left by the gent as had the room before you.

Mrs. Bellamy. — Boots! Where?

(Voice.) — Hunder the window-curting, ma'am.

Mrs. Bellamy. — Boots! Curtain!

(She rushes to curtain, draws it aside, picks up boots, carries one in each hand to the center of the stage, and stands, flourishing them.)

Saved! Saved! *(Runs to door, throws out boots.)* Here, my good man, take your boots. What a frightful adventure! I never shall get over it. One thing is certain: from this time forth I shall go nowhere alone. To provide for all contingencies, to-morrow at eleven I accept that dear, big, brave Fitzhenry.

Curtain.

TEA AT FOUR O'CLOCK

A DRAWING-ROOM COMEDY
IN ONE ACT

CHARACTERS:

MRS. EFFINGHAM,	. . . *A young widow.*
MRS. MARABOUT,	. . . *An emotional female.*
MRS. CODDINGTON,	. . { *A mamma with a daughter to bring out.*
ARABELLA CODDINGTON,	. . *A girl with nothing to say.*
ARTHUR RUTLEDGE,	. . *An innocent offender.*
WALTON,	. . . . . . *A social cynic.*
GRAYSON,	. . . . . . *A tender and true young man.*
APPLEBY,	. . . . . . *A can't-get-it-out young man.*
SABRETACHE,	. . . . . *A thunder-and-Mars young man.*
DR. GRANTLEY,	. . . . *A professional button-holer.*
THOMAS,	. . . . . . *A footman.*

THE SCENE IS IN A NEW-YORK DRAWING-ROOM
TIME, THE PRESENT
MODERN MORNING DRESS

TEA AT FOUR O'CLOCK was first seen at private houses in Lenox and in New York. It was presented, after much rehearsal, at the Madison Square Theatre matinées, January 13th and 14th, 1887. This play requires brisk action and perfect knowledge of the lines. It should, therefore, not be put on hastily to fill a gap in some programme. Where so many actors are at once upon the stage, each having a character part to sustain, there is no hope of success without faithful preliminary

drill. The scene is a drawing-room of modern days, furnished luxuriously; the costumes those in ordinary use on the occasion of afternoon visits. The men wear frock-coats and carry hats and sticks. The ladies, except Mrs. Effingham who wears demi-toilette, are in street costume with wraps and bonnets. Palms, screens, etc., scattered about the scene are useful in affording opportunities for "business," the dramatis personæ changing places from time to time to avoid stiffness in their grouping.

TEA AT FOUR O'CLOCK.

SCENE: *A fashionable drawing-room. Thomas in the act of reading a newspaper. In one hand he holds a feather duster, in the other a Dresden figurine, which falls to the ground with a crash. Thomas stoops to pick it up, with a grimace.*

THOMAS.— Bad luck to ye now, for a murtherin' blag-guard, to slip atween me fingers like that. Sure, an' me lady ought to know better at her time o' life, and she a widdy woman, to go temptin' a pore fellow's fingers wid scatterin' the chaney around, for all the wurrld like a musayum. I'll be blist av there 's a table convaynient to lay the duster on, while I do be readin' me marnin' Hirald. And what 'll I do wid the payces ? Here 's his head, the spalpeen. He 's squintin' at me! Och, for sure, I 'll be after clappin' it in me pocket, and the misthress 'll never be the wiser. Faith, an' it 's grateful to me she might be, wid such a lot o' them imidges as I ain't broken yet.

(Enter Mrs. Effingham in reception toilet, R.)

MRS. EFFINGHAM.— What, Thomas, not ready yet! How often have I told you that you *must* be in livery before three o'clock on Mondays! *(Catching sight of fragments on carpet.)* What is that? An arm of my lovely Dresden figurine, that I paid such a price for only a week ago!

THOMAS *(scratching his head).*— Sure, mum, it 's an arrum, or a leg, or a head. I 'm that flustered wid misfortune, I can't adzackly make out which.

(Picks it up and hands it to Mrs. Effingham.)

MRS. EFFINGHAM.— And where, if I may ask, is the rest of it?

THOMAS *(taking pieces from pocket).*— Here, ma'am. I was just considerin' av it could be rightly mended; but if ye 'd take my advice, ye 'd discard him altogether, the cross-eyed spalpeen!

MRS. EFFINGHAM.— And you intended to omit the arm in restoration?

THOMAS.— I was only takin' pattern by the artist that made yer statoo of the Vaynus. I 'll be afther tellin' ye, ma'am, the way the accident occurred. I was only aisin' me mind by reading the marnin' paper, like this— And the butt end of my duster went whack, like this—

(Suits action to words, with same result as before; another figurine is smashed. Thomas aghast.)

MRS. EFFINGHAM.— Enough, Thomas; you will ruin me. I am forced to give you warning.

THOMAS.— Och, ma'am, an it 's not the Christian lady ye are that 'd be turnin' a pore b'ye away widout a karracter, an' all on account of his family troubles, when it 's nearly kilt I am wid just thryin' to live, avick! Thrue as ye 're born, ma'am, it 's from me grandfather in the ould country I got it, and he, pore man,— God rest his soul,— died of it, forbye the doctors, and an illigant funeral he had, as 'ud be a satisfaction to any corpse. It's a sort of a kind of a jerking spasm, that takes me all unbeknownst when I do be not in the laste prepared.

MRS. EFFINGHAM *(laughing).* — Go, now, Thomas, and get yourself in condition to attend the door, at once.

> *(Exit Thomas, holding the fragments of figurine in his hand. He apostrophizes them in dumb show behind Mrs. Effingham.)*

MRS. EFFINGHAM *(drawing on her gloves, and walking to and fro to arrange chairs, lamps, flowers, etc.).* — Well, here I am, booked to stay in-doors on this lovely Spring day when I would like nothing better than a turn in the park! What a nuisance one's day at home becomes! The right people never come in when they are expected, or if they do't is only to run into the wrong people. I believe I'm getting cynical. How strange it is! At fifteen one believes in eternal youth; one mocks at the grim wolf, middle age, as he growls from afar. So the years drift on, till some fine morning one wakes up to confront the first wrinkle — the tiny foreshadowing of a wrinkle — a pencil sketch to be inked hereafter! *(Looks nervously about her.)* I have seen it just here *(touches cheek with forefinger),* and *(in a melancholy tone)* soon every one will see it! *(She drops into easy chair.)* Ah! how long this afternoon will seem! Not a soul I care to see, of course. A stream of dull people, and I, smiling here, bowing there, pouring out tea, protesting I am enchanted, when I am bored, bored, bored to death! I can't understand why Arthur did n't come yesterday; not so much as a note or a bunch of violets. I was so cold on Saturday when he said good-bye. His eyes had that deep, wounded, yearning look! No, he will never come on my day at home, that's certain; he detests gossiping people. Ah! *(rising and walking about)* society is a prison into which we are cast, as soon as we

are born, and in vain we cry, "We can't get out!" Alas!
*(She sighs deeply, then catching sight of her reflection in the
mirror, a complete change of manner ensues.)* I thought so, and
now I'm sure of it! *(Works her arm about in sleeve.)* This
is the last dress she shall ever have from me, the horrid
little fraud. That abominable Clementine *has simply
ruined my back!*

(Bell.)

Ah! one of my jailers, I presume.

THOMAS *(withdrawing a portière, announces).*—Misther
Grayson. *(Exit.)*

(Enter Grayson.)

MRS. EFFINGHAM.—Mr. Grayson! This is an unexpected
pleasure, to welcome one of your sex so early in the day.
To what happy chance do I owe it?

GRAYSON.—To no chance, I assure you. I've latterly
failed so often to see you, that I have made a bold effort to
be your very first visitor to-day. *(Seats himself at her side.)*
In fact, I've so generally been too late, it is a comfort to
find myself for once too soon.

MRS. EFFINGHAM *(unfurling fan).*—Don't think my remark meant a reproach. You know you are always welcome.

GRAYSON *(aside).*—Too cordial by half. But now that
I'm here, I must seize my opportunity. *(Aloud, putting down
hat and stick.)* Dear Mrs. Effingham, if you could only
understand what these delays and obstacles are to a man
in my tortured state of mind! Be gracious, be compassion-
ate, and say that you will hear me!

MRS. EFFINGHAM *(aside).*—I'm afraid I'm in for it.
(Aloud.) One couldn't be anything but gracious on such
a heavenly day, Mr. Grayson. *(Rising and going to window,
R.)* Oh, what an elastic atmosphere. Really, it is almost
warm, don't you think so?

GRAYSON *(ruefully picking up hat and stick).*—Not at all;
I find it cool, decidedly.

MRS. EFFINGHAM *(arranging flowers in window-box)*. — My mignonette will soon be in bloom. Do you know, Mr. Grayson, I can't imagine anybody, who *can* be out-of-doors to-day, being willing to remain within.

GRAYSON. — I refuse to take the hint. Your presence, Mrs. Effingham, makes perpetual sunshine.

MRS. EFFINGHAM. — What pretty things you always say, Mr. Grayson — to everybody, don't you ?

GRAYSON. — Crushed again ! Yes, as you were saying, the weather is fine, certainly—very fine ; I—ah—venture to assert, without fear of contradiction, that I never knew it finer !

MRS. EFFINGHAM. — Such a long, dull winter as we are having ! Don't you find it very dull, Mr. Grayson ? *(Suppresses yawn.)* I do.

GRAYSON. — Hum ! ha ! *(Aside.)* She shan't get the better of me, I'll swear ! When a man has a declaration on the tip of his tongue he's a fool if he lets slip an opportunity like this ! *(Aloud.)* My dear Mrs. Effingham ! Adorable Lilian ! If ever there were a man whose love for you is true, intense, overmastering, it is ——

(Bell.)

THOMAS *(withdrawing portière)*. — Misther Walton !

> *(Enter Walton. Exit Thomas. Grayson, disgusted, takes up hat and stick and goes to window, R.)*

GRAYSON *(aside)*. — That fool, Walton !

WALTON *(aside)*. — That idiot, Grayson !

> *(They salute each other frigidly.)*

MRS. EFFINGHAM. — Mr. Walton ! I thought you were in Wyoming or Arizona — some one of those buffalo and Indian places men escape to nowadays.

WALTON. — And so I have been ; just as far away from you as I could conveniently go.

MRS. EFFINGHAM *(languidly)*. — Thanks, very much, I'm sure.

Walton.— But we wanderers come back to New York for civilization, as whales come to the surface for air.

Mrs. Effingham.— Of course, you are brimful of adventures. Pray tell me the most exciting thing that happened all the time you were away.

Walton.— Willingly. For one thing, I got married. *You* would not have me, and so, finding consolation elsewhere, I jumped headlong into matrimony, as a harlequin goes through a trap.

Grayson *(aside)*.— Married, by jove! Hurrah!

(He comes forward.)

Mrs. Effingham *(indifferently)*.— Married! I congratulate you.

Walton.— That is to say, I was married; very much married — utterly married. But I'm not at all so now, thank you. I'm a despairing widower.

Grayson *(dejectedly, aside)*.— The devil he is! *(Aloud.)* I say, Walton, does that sort of luck — ahem! — I mean, blow — often happen to a fellow so soon in married life?

Walton.— I see how you feel for me, my dear fellow. Thank you for your sympathy in my grief.

Grayson *(who has been smiling, endeavors to be gloomy)*.— I? Oh — ah — yes! Pray believe in my deepest commiseration.

Mrs. Effingham *(handkerchief to eyes)*.— And in mine.

Walton.— Restrain your emotion, my good friends; keep it for a more worthy object. I am afraid I made a fiasco in that little venture. Strange! Everybody knows what a sweet-tempered, biddable, affectionate kind of creature I am. *She* was reputed to be an angel. And yet, marriage is like an experiment in chemistry. Unite two harmless drugs and you have a deadly poison.

Grayson *(sentimentally glancing at widow)*.— But then yours was not a *love* match, Walton.

WALTON. — Love! What, are you Arcadian enough to still believe in that exploded myth?

MRS. EFFINGHAM. — Was there ever anything so odd as the way people have of drifting into this kind of talk? No matter what point the conversation starts from, it always ends in ——

WALTON *(cynically).* —
MRS. EFFINGHAM *(satirically).* — } Love!
GRAYSON *(tenderly).* —

MRS. EFFINGHAM. — Come, Mr. Grayson, you are a believer. Give us a good definition of the tender passion. *(Aside.)* One must find something to say.

> *(She seats herself on sofa. Grayson leans over it from behind. Walton stands, back to mantelpiece.)*

GRAYSON *(aside).* — Another opportunity. *(Aloud.)* Willingly, Mrs. Effingham. You inspire me to eloquence — you loosen the flood-gates — you uncurb the torrents, that, lava-like ——

MRS. EFFINGHAM *(interposing her fan).* — Ah! I beseech you, Mr. Grayson, no volcanoes; no torrents — nothing violent or exciting. Give us a nice, comfortable, easygoing, jog-trot sort of an emotion.

GRAYSON *(discomfited, aside).* — H-um, h-a-h! This is not what I call easy-going. Devil take the woman. *(Aloud.)* Love, my dear Mrs. Effingham, is perhaps most briefly described as embodied in ——

> *(Bell.)*

THOMAS *(withdrawing portière).* — Misther Appleby!

> *(Exit Thomas. Grayson makes a gesture of impatience; crosses stage to examine pictures, etc.)*

WALTON. — What, Appleby, the miser millionaire, enrolled among your slaves! Truly, he is a formidable rival. 'T is said he is even saving of his words, which accounts for his never being able to complete a sentence.

MRS. EFFINGHAM *(with lifted forefinger).* — Hush! he is here!

> *(Enter Appleby. He advances to meet hostess, who rises, then resumes her seat. Appleby sits on sofa at her side, L.)*

APPLEBY. — Mrs. Ef-Ef-Ef-ingham! Mr. Grayson! Mr. Walton! *(To Walton.)* I have n't had the pleasure since we cr-cr-crossed together in the Gug-Gug-Gug——

MRS. EFFINGHAM *(rapidly).* — Delightful ship, is n't she? I never take any other if I can help it. As you came in, Mr. Appleby, Mr. Grayson was just giving us his definition of love. No one would ever believe how eloquent and clever he can be! *(Grayson winces.)* Pray continue, Mr. Grayson.

GRAYSON *(stiffly).* — You will excuse me, Mrs. Effingham; the thread of my ideas was too suddenly snapped.

WALTON. — Will you accept my definition, instead?

MRS. EFFINGHAM. — Something chemical, I suppose?

WALTON. — Love is an airy nothing — a thistledown that a breath may blow away! In brief, a ——

> *(Bell.)*

THOMAS. — Misthress Marabout!

> *(Enter Mrs. Marabout. Exit Thomas.)*

MRS. EFFINGHAM *(rising and coming forward).* — How do you do, my dear? So good of you not to forget my Mondays. *(Aside.)* Just came to show her new Worth wrap. *(Aloud.)* Pray sit down and throw aside your cloak. You 'll find it oppressive in this warm room. *(Offers to remove Mrs. M.'s cloak.)*

MRS. MARABOUT *(resisting and out of breath.)* — Not at all, my dear; I 'm always a little chilly, you know. *(Looks around for a fan, takes up Chinese fire-screen and fans herself violently.)* How pretty your rooms are, and how charmingly you 're dressed; but you 're pale, are n't you — or else a little thin? Worn out, perhaps, with keeping too late hours?

MRS. EFFINGHAM *(aside)*.—That 's the civil for saying I 'm a fright. *(Aloud.)* We are not all so successful in preserving our looks as long as you do, dear. By the way, your wrap is really *very* nice. I had n't noticed it before. I had no idea Clementine could do so well.

MRS. MARABOUT · *(sharply)*. — Clementine, indeed! Worth's last, my dear; and I should think you would know the difference! *(Fans herself.)*

MRS. EFFINGHAM *(smoothly)*.— Worth! I would n't have imagined it. Tea, Thomas! And, Thomas, Mrs. Marabout finds the room is cool; poke the fire.

> *(As Thomas increases the blaze Mrs. Marabout walks away, R., fanning herself with increasing vigor.)*

WALTON *(following her, R.)*.— Pray, let me relieve you. *(Takes fan.)*

> *(Grayson and Appleby stand near Mrs. Effingham and converse with her. Enter Thomas with tea-table, which he places by Mrs. Effingham; afterward brings in tea-tray, fashionably equipped. Mrs. Effingham makes tea.)*

THOMAS *(going out, shows broken cup)*.— Musha, it 's lucky then, the quality don't count their dozens. She 'll never be afther knowin' that I 've just sint one of them egg-shell tay-cups to kape company with the broken imidges.

> *(Exit Thomas.)*

MRS. MARABOUT.— So nice to see you back again, Mr. Walton. I quite envy you that delightful unconventional life you have been leading. A more primitive state of society than ours would be just what I would choose. There used to be a poem when I learned lessons, about Lo! the poor Indian, whose something — mind — I forget the rest. If a few thousand persons moving in society could only go and be Indians, I would put down my name directly. But, moving in society, unfortunately we can't.

WALTON.— An enormous loss to the Indians, madam.

MRS. MARABOUT.— I often say to my husband that I am utterly unsuited to the cold atmosphere of conventional life. Such a child of nature ; the weakest of creatures — my feelings touched in a moment. Yes, sugar, please; and cream, Mr. Appleby. *(She sips tea which Appleby crosses to hand her.)* Often and often I sob for hours together, for no reason in the world.

WALTON *(aside)*.— Uncommonly cheerful for Marabout, I swear. *(Aloud.)* Highly interesting for the doctors, is it not ?

MRS. MARABOUT.— Doctors ! Don't speak to me of doctors ! I've baffled them all ! One of my pet peculiarities is an objection to the smell of certain flowers. Hyacinths, for instance, make me faint. *(Looks about her and sees vase on table.)* I would wager anything there is a hyacinth in that vase yonder. Oh, this terrible oppression ! — water ! — eau de cologne ! — anything ! — all grows dark before me.

> *(She droops. Walton, with a gesture of dismay, receives her in his arms.)*

WALTON *(aside)*.— For a creature all sensibility she 's no light weight. *(Places her on sofa.)*

> *(All surround Mrs. Marabout. Mrs. Effingham applies usual remedies. Appleby seizes the milk-jug, but is prevented from throwing its contents on the sufferer. Grayson, with vague idea of burnt feathers, brings dust brush from the hearth. As the invalid revives Mrs. Effingham brings near the vase of flowers, hiding them behind her.)*

MRS. EFFINGHAM. — Are you relieved now, dear, and you are quite sure it was the scent of those naughty hyacinths ?

MRS. MARABOUT (*faintly*).— Oh! that fatal hyacinth! O Lilian, what would I give for nerves like yours!

MRS. EFFINGHAM (*distinctly*). — My nerves *are* proof against hyacinths, I confess; especially when they are made of muslin. (*She shows the vase.*) Artificial, my dear Julie, as you see!

> (*All laugh. Confusion of Mrs. Marabout. Bell.*)

THOMAS (*withdrawing the portière*). — Mistress Coddington and Miss Coddington!

> (*Exit Thomas. Enter Mrs. Coddington and her daughter; they greet hostess and cross, R.*)

MRS. CODDINGTON (*to daughter, aside*).— Now, Arabella, mind what I say, and whatever you do, don't let the conversation flag; keep the ball moving; be gay, sprightly, artless, agreeable, and suave.

ARABELLA (*helplessly, aside*).— But if I 've nothing to say, mamma?

MRS. CODDINGTON (*sharply, aside*). — Nothing to say, forsooth! Nothing to say! And how dare you presume, miss, to have nothing to say? Keep your wits about you, miss, or when we get home again, I 'll have something to say!

> (*Conversation around tea-table. Appleby has repeatedly consulted his watch, is about to take his leave.*)

WALTON (*to Mrs. Effingham, aside*). — What the deuce is Appleby always looking at his watch for? I have it! He has taken a cab by the hour.

MRS. EFFINGHAM. — Oh, you malicious creature! We can only hope his hour has come at last!

WALTON. — What fun, to plunge him into the extravagance of another hour of cab hire!

> (*As Appleby just then approaches to say adieu, Walton slips his arm within Appleby's confidingly.*)

WALTON. — Appleby, did I ever tell you that adventure of mine in the Rockies last August ?

(*Walton leads Appleby apart, extreme L. Appleby's watch drops back into his pocket and with manifest effort he resigns himself.*)

MRS. EFFINGHAM (*pleasantly*). — I hope you have enjoyed your drive this afternoon, Miss Coddington ?

(*Arabella, much alarmed, drops card-case, scattering cards. Appleby tries to pick them up ; their heads meet and bump.*)

MRS. CODDINGTON (*to daughter with a jog, aside*). — Speak up, you awkward thing ! Be lively, bright, be unstudied — artless as a fawn — a greenwood fawn !

ARABELLA (*with a desperate effort, aside*). — How can I be like a fawn, mamma, when you glare at me like that. (*To Mrs. Effingham.*) Yes, Mrs. Effingham, not at all ; that is, very much, thanks. (*Aside.*) Oh, dear, I hate society. She told me to say anything that came into my head. *Nothing* comes into my head but that I 'd like to drown myself. Mamma's elbow will jog me black and blue before she 's done. (*Aloud.*) Yes, Mrs. Effingham, if you please, we drove out in the park — Central Park — yes, that was the very park. Something came near happening as we passed the Museum — yes, the Museum. It was a sea-lion that had escaped and was running down the drive.

ALL. — A sea-lion !

(*Arabella, much confused, drops cards again. Appleby again stoops, she stoops, their heads meet, Arabella finding all eyes upon her.*)

ARABELLA. — I mean a gazelle, or perhaps a crazy man ; at all events, policemen took it to the station-house, and it kicked — oh ! how it kicked and swore — yes, swore dreadfully ! Oh ! ——

WALTON (*taps his forehead, aside, to Appleby*). — Light in the upper story, eh ?

MRS. CODDINGTON *(hastily).*— My daughter and I have just had the pleasure of visiting the Sybarites' new club-house. What luxury! What extravagance! Think of men spending all that money on a place where women can't be with them! I 'll vow it is a mystery how marriages are ever made nowadays. The Sybarites is a premium on celibacy.

APPLEBY *(watch in hand, makes a fresh start. He crosses room).*— T-t-t-hat reminds me — reminds me, Mrs. Effing-ham, that I 'm d-due at the c-cl-club at ——

MRS. EFFINGHAM *(glancing mischievously at Walton).*— I protest against your desertion, Mr. Appleby; not, at any rate, before I have had the pleasure of presenting you to my friends. Mrs. and Miss Coddington — Mr. Appleby.

> *(Appleby's watch falls in pocket; he resigns him-self again.)*

MRS. CODDINGTON *(aside).*— Appleby, the millionaire; the match of the season. What a delightful coincidence that he and Arabella should have bumped each other's heads. That 's what I call purely providential. Arabella, child, don't poke your chin out; think of something clever to say upon the spot. Be sportive, and sparkling as the dew-drop on the rose, and mind what I say, miss: remember you 're on no account to let the conversation flag.

ARABELLA *(aside).*— I have n't the ghost of an idea; I 'm cold to my very toes, she frightens me so. It 's like speak-ing a piece on Fridays before the school.

MRS. EFFINGHAM.— So you visited the Sybarites, Miss Coddington,— that fountain-head of gossip,— and brought away no news?

ARABELLA *(goaded by a glance and a nudge from Mrs. Coddington).*— Yes, Mrs. Effingham, there was news of something dreadful. It was — yes, I believe it was a murder — no, a duel ——

ALL.— A duel at the Sybarites!

ARABELLA *(hurriedly).*— A desperate duel of the worst kind between two — two adversaries. It was likely both would be killed at once, or one immediately after the other. Yes, both killed! Really dead, you know. They had gone away from town to fight. Yes, away, quite away, from town.

MRS. EFFINGHAM *(speaking languidly).*— To Maryland, I suppose; that classic ground. But pray tell us the names of the combatants, Miss Coddington. You pique our curiosity.

ARABELLA *(holding down her head).* — It was — Captain Hartshorn, I believe; — yes, Captain Hartshorn, and they vowed to kill each other without the slightest intermission.

MRS. EFFINGHAM *(still languidly).* — But his adversary? Don't leave us in such painful expectation.

ARABELLA *(hesitating, aside).*— His adversary. Oh! must he have an adversary? Who *shall* I say? *(Aloud.)* It was Mr. Rutledge, I think; — yes, Arthur Rutledge, and I don't know anything more about it, I'm sure — not if you tease and tease me ever so much. *(She bursts into tears.)*

MRS. CODDINGTON *(horrified).*— Arabella! But what is the matter with dear Mrs. Effingham?

> *(Mrs. Effingham starts violently, utters a faint scream, half rises from her chair, sinks into it again and lets fall her cup; cup breaks; Grayson and Walton exchange glances of astonishment.)*

MRS. EFFINGHAM *(aside).* — Rutledge — Arthur! Great Heaven! Fighting! Wounded perhaps —— *(She rings bell.)*
> *(Enter Thomas.)*

MRS. EFFINGHAM.— Thomas!

THOMAS.— Yes, ma'am.

MRS. EFFINGHAM.— I rang for you.

THOMAS.— Sure, an' it 's meself that he's answerin' ye, ma'am.

(Mrs. Effingham goes to left of stage. Thomas follows her.)

MRS. EFFINGHAM.— I want you to go — to send — to call a cab, a messenger, immediately, to — *(Aside.)* Oh, no ; I dare not ! How hopelessly foolish of me even to dream of it ! *(She ponders.)*

THOMAS *(puzzled)*.— It 's to call a cab, an' to call a messenger, and pl'ase, ma'am, is the cab to go in the messenger and where 's he to go to when he gets there ?

MRS. EFFINGHAM *(starting from reverie)*.— Pick up the bits of that cup, and bring hot water. *(Aside.)* My place is here, chained to the wheel, while he is madly throwing away his precious life in this desperate encounter. *(Crosses back to tea-table.)*

THOMAS *(carefully collecting fragments of cup)*.— And to think of the mistress herself turned butter-fingers ! Howly Mither o' Moses, but is n't this a consolation to an innicent offinder !

(Bell. Exit Thomas.)

MRS. EFFINGHAM *(aside)*.— And I let him go without the fond, foolish words that were ever trembling on my tongue, but that I dared not utter.

THOMAS *(drawing portière)*.— Gineral Sabretache !

(Exit Thomas. Sabretache enters swaggering.)

SABRETACHE.— My compliments to you, Mrs. Effingham ! Ladies, good morning !

MRS. MARABOUT.— Good-bye, Lilian, I really must be off. Six teas still on my list, and I 'm dying to drop in on Fanny Golightly to see how she takes the news of Rutledge's affair. You know that everybody is saying she and Rutledge are engaged. Shall I tell her, dear, she has your sympathy ? Good-bye, dearest ; keep your spirits up !

Mrs. Effingham. — Good-bye, dearest ! *(Aside.)* Horrid little cat !

> *(Exit Mrs. Marabout. Appleby is about to follow her, when Walton interrupts him by an introduction in dumb show to General Sabretache, who greets him with effusion, squeezes his hand until Appleby winces, and takes Appleby's arm in his. Grayson, Mrs. Coddington, Miss Coddington form group, L. Mrs. Effingham at tea table. General Sabretache, Walton, Appleby, R.*

Walton.— You are just in time, General, to shed the light of experience on our discussion. Duels and dueling ; testimony by an expert ; startling facts in evidence ; broadswords and blunderbusses, eh ! And champion shots — from a very long bow.

Mrs. Effingham *(with an effort)*.— Pray do, General Sabretache ; it will be so amusing.

Sabretache *(fiercely)*.— Amusing ! Not so, madam ; astonishing, exciting, awe-inspiring, if you will, but not amusing. I *never* amuse. The book of my experience is writ in characters of b-lood !

Mrs. Effingham *(shudders, then recovers herself, aside)*. — I am a woman ! Let me hide this from their eyes. *(Aloud.)* Then pray go on, and be as terrible as you choose.

Sabretache.— The toy of inexorable destiny, I have been from my cradle compelled to dabble without ceasing in human gore. At Chickamauga and at Gettysburg, at Sadowa and Sedan, at Plevna and Alexandria, the name of Sabretache may be found inscribed upon the highest roll of honor. And not in the tented field alone. Affairs of honor — pooh ! mere bagatelles ! I 've had 'em by the score — at Paris, at Hamburg, in Vienna, in New York. Once resolved upon the fall of my opponent, his doom is sealed. A case in point ?

You shall have it. My little adventure in Paris — the affair Solomon, I call it. I was lounging in the garden of the Palais Royal, my dog at my feet. A gentleman, in passing, was inconsiderate enough to tread on the tail of my dog; my dog howled. I remarked to the offender, " Sir, a dog is the friend of humanity. Sir, you have stepped on the tail of my friend — mark you, *my* friend. Sir, you will apologize to my friend." If you will believe me, he refused. He even went so far as to say, "D——n your friend!" Of course there was but one alternative. I offered him the sword —— *(Sabretache stops, glares, twirls his mustache.)*

MRS. EFFINGHAM.—And the end of it all, Colonel Sabretache, was ——

SABRETACHE *(ominously).* — What would you have, madam? The man apologized, so to speak — went down upon his knees to Solomon.

APPLEBY.— S-S-S-S-S-olomon!

SABRETACHE *(fiercely).*—My dog's name, Mr. Appleby, was Solomon! S-o, *So,* l-o, *lo,* m-o-n, *mon,*— Solomon! Perhaps you don't approve of it?

APPLEBY *(shrinking at every syllable).*— P-p-p-perfectly so, my dear sir; I don't recall a more appropriate title for a do-og — a fr-fri-friend, I should say; a friend. Really, Mrs. Effingham, I must —— *(Consulting watch.)*

MRS. EFFINGHAM.— I was just about asking you to ring the bell for me. *(Aside.)* I must do something; but what?

> *(Appleby's chance lost ; his watch drops in pocket ; he rings bell. Enter Thomas.)*

MRS. EFFINGHAM *(walking to extreme left).*— Thomas, I have an order for you. *(Aside.)* You will go immediately —send immediately — to the lodgings of Mr. Rutledge. Say that his — his maiden aunt is in town, and wishes to know whether there is news of him. *(Aloud.)* See to the fire.

THOMAS *(aside)*.—Sure, an' it 's meself knows the road to the gintleman's, when it 's paved both ways with silver shillings.

> *(Thomas kneels before fire arranging it. Mrs. Effing-*
> *ham crosses, R., to jardinière. Grayson follows her.*
> *They stand talking.)*

WALTON.— You have given us an interesting account — a bloodless victory, General Sabretache. Is there nothing more recent ?

SABRETACHE *(mysteriously)*. — Nothing, sir ? Too much — I dare not reveal all in the presence of lovely woman.

> *(Bows and waves his hand. Mrs. Coddington curtsies.)*

MISS CODDINGTON *(aside)*. — Here, mamma, is a gentle-man who does not let the conversation flag.

MRS. CODDINGTON *(aside)*. — Take example by him, my dear. A most agreeable talker, and so exciting.

SABRETACHE. — Latterly, I was at the theater. A man persisted in staring at me; an oblique gaze. Striding toward him I demanded the meaning of that gaze. Some men with him were audacious enough to take his part. Idiots ! in ten minutes, instead of one affair upon my hands, I had four.

MRS. CODDINGTON. — Four !

ARABELLA *(following suit)*. — Four !

WALTON *(aside)*. — Why in the world did n't he make it fourteen, while he was about it ?

SABRETACHE *(swaggering up and down)*.— We met on the appointed day. In less than half an hour I had broken the arm of one antagonist, the thigh of another, the collar-bone of number three. A-a-h !

MRS. CODDINGTON.—And the fourth, poor soul ! what became of him ?

ARABELLA *(imitating)*. — Yes, what became of him ?

SABRETACHE.—Just here occurred a most extraordinary circumstance. I had abandoned the pistol for the sword.

Naturally there was no hope for my opponent, who, by the way, was the man who stared at me. But, with my usual generosity, I resolved to spare his life.

MRS. CODDINGTON *(raising her hands).* — How truly great of you! *(Aside to Arabella.)* Speak up, Arabella.

> *(Arabella, aroused from reverie, starts, drops cards. Appleby picks them up; their heads bump. Arabella rises in confusion, and looking about her, says to Appleby —" How truly great of you!")*

SABRETACHE. — Was n't it? I had resolved only to strike the sword from his hand. Observe what follows. My stroke was so neat that his sword, lifted high into the air, turned thrice and descended, piercing my ill-fated adversary thro' the eye — of course, instantly killing him. A-a-ah!

MRS. CODDINGTON. — How superbly heroic! Arabella thinks so too, don't you, Arabella?

SABRETACHE. — So it was, madam. But the cream of the joke is that, when all was over, I discovered the fellow meant nothing at all by his oblique intensity — he squinted.

THOMAS *(who has been loitering under pretense of brushing hearth, etc., aside).* — For the wurrld and all, like me chaney imidge.

MRS. EFFINGHAM *(perceiving him, and crossing from jardinière).* — What, Thomas! not gone yet? *(Aside.)* How can I endure this anxiety one moment longer. *(Aloud.)* And pray, what do you mean by loitering here?

WALTON. — He was waiting for the death of the General's fourth victim. *(Exit Thomas, with a grin.)* Positively, Sabretache, you inspire me to recall some of my own warlike experiences; not that I have anything worth telling, after you.

MRS. EFFINGHAM *(aside).* — How persistently they hover round this subject. *(Aloud.)* Mr. Walton, of that you will permit your audience to be the judge.

MRS. CODDINGTON. — Yes, do, Mr. Walton.

ARABELLA *(aside, to her mother).* — Here is somebody else who does n't want to talk, mamma.

MRS. CODDINGTON *(aside).* — Stupid! of course he does. Wait a minute and see.

WALTON *(with affected hesitation).* — Well, well, since you insist upon it; but my achievement is a feeble gas-jet, beside the General's Brush-electric. It was during the late war, when I commanded a company of cavalry in Virginia. I rode out before breakfast, with my orderly, saw smoke issuing from the chimney of a disused cabin, rode softly up, dismounted, peeped thro' the chinks, saw a round dozen of desperate fellows,—Mosby's best men, — armed to the teeth and sitting at breakfast with bowie-knives beside each plate, and muskets laid across their knees. Without a moment's hesitation I uttered a terrific war-cry and placed myself at the threshold with extended sword. Believing themselves surrounded, the black horsemen dashed to the door. Single-handed I met them and after a long and bloody conflict, eleven of them bit the dust.

SABRETACHE *(with an air of mortification).* — Eleven!

WALTON *(calmly).* — I was a trifle out of breath, and my arm had lost a little of its terrible dash, and so the twelfth ——

MRS. EFFINGHAM. — Ran away, I suppose.

WALTON. — Far from it; you never were more mistaken. The twelfth cavalryman rallied ferociously and — *(imitating Sabretache)* — killed me on the spot.

> *(He laughs. All laugh*
> *but Sabretache, who*
> *frowns blackly.)*

SABRETACHE. — I don't know what you call it, Mr. Walton, but this appears to me to be a very poor joke.

WALTON. — Joke! It was a serious matter to me, I assure you. I never dreamt of disputing your feat with your squinting adversary, General. I beg of you to show equal respect to my untimely death.

SABRETACHE *(making his adieu to Mrs. Effingham).*— Your servant, madam. You, Mr. Walton, shall hear from me anon — anon, sir! A-a-ah!

(Exit Sabretache.)

MRS. CODDINGTON *(alarmed).*— Oh, Mr. Walton, how could you tempt that desperate character! I tremble at the danger that may be in store for you.

WALTON.— Never fear, madam. An encounter with the valiant Sabretache is a brevet of immortality. I wish my friend Rutledge were as safe in his affair. Hartshorn, it is said, is a crack shot. *(He watches the effect on Mrs. Effingham.)*

MRS. EFFINGHAM *(hysterically).*— Mr. Grayson, you are the most obliging of mortals; if you would only go to the club and fetch us the very latest news of this affair of poor Mr. Rutledge! We're all *so* interested!

GRAYSON.— At your command, "I'll put a girdle round the earth in forty minutes."

(Exit Grayson.)

WALTON *(calling after him).*— Take Appleby's cab, Grayson, you'll make better time.

(Bell.)

APPLEBY *(starts, looking anxiously at watch).*— I would volunteer with p-p-pleasure, Mrs. Effingham, but that it is impossible f-f-for me to return. I shall really be obliged to s-s-s-say ——

THOMAS *(announcing).*— Dr. Grantley!

MRS. EFFINGHAM.— Arthur's uncle!

WALTON.— That long-winded old Grantley, who is forever talking about the tariff!

MRS. EFFINGHAM.— He has come to tell me all. Heaven give me strength to bear it.

(Enter Dr. Grantley.)

DR. GRANTLEY.— Good-day, madam, good-day! Fine
weather we are having!

MRS. EFFINGHAM.— Oh, Doctor, don't dissemble! Don't
try to hide it! I have divined the object of your visit.

DR. GRANTLEY.— The object of my visit!

MRS. EFFINGHAM.— Go away, please, and talk to some
one else. Only say that you don't despise my weakness.

DR. GRANTLEY.— Despise your weakness!

MRS. EFFINGHAM.— How could you, though, considering
how dear the object is to both of us.

DR. GRANTLEY.— Hum! haw! To both of us?

MRS. EFFINGHAM.— Go, leave me. Already curious eyes
are turned upon us.

> *(Mrs. Coddington and Arabella draw*
> *near; she introduces him to both.)*

WALTON. — Appleby, I'll make common cause with you.
I'll share your cab. By hard driving, your man may
reach the club inside of the two hours.

APPLEBY. — Two hours, at a dollar and a half an hour, is
pretty deuced s-s-s-t——

WALTON. — Steep. Excuse me, but I've no time to
spare. See, he is coming toward us. Cling to me, Appleby,
or I am lost.

DR. GRANTLEY. — Walton! Appleby! The very men I
have been looking for, to talk about the tariff. *(Takes an*
arm of each and leads them down, R.) I can't think how I
managed to lose you at the club last night, Walton, just
after I had promised to read you that little article of mine,
prepared for the "Evening Post." Appleby, too — a man
of capital and one of our representative citizens; you will
be interested in my views of the important question. Come,
now, there's no time like the present, and while our good
hostess is making herself agreeable to her other friends,
just let me give you a few of my leading points. I have
my manuscript here in my pocket. No trouble! No trouble,

I assure you. I like to oblige my friends. *(Draws immensely thick paper from pocket, puts on spectacles, and, with hems and haws, reads.)* "The paramount purpose of a tariff should be to provide for the expenses of Government by taxes which so distribute themselves as to be not only indirect, but least burdensome upon the industries of the country. If special industries are fostered, the protection afforded should be incidental only"— incidental, you observe ——

WALTON. — Yes, incidental. Exactly. So I should have said.

DR. GRANTLEY *(resumes)*. — "And the law-maker should never consider his duty performed when he enriches a few at the expense of all."

APPLEBY. — That's j-j-just what you're doing to us, doctor, don't you see? Why d-d-don't you enrich 'em all?

DR. GRANTLEY. — There are moments, sir, when a joke is out of place. However, as you and Walton seem interested, I'll go on. This paragraph, now, will take your fancy. Hum! haw! "The present tariff is an iniquity for which the circumstances of the present situation afford no justification whatever. In reforming it, the free list should be immediately enlarged by a long catalogue of raw materials."

(During this Walton and Appleby steal away.)

MRS. EFFINGHAM. — He is taking out a paper. No doubt a telegram. Yes, dear Mrs. Coddington, of course, you may put me down.

MRS. CODDINGTON *(subscription book in hand)*. — So kind of you, Mrs. Effingham. Fifty dollars, did you say? What good news for my committee! I'll try for a subscription from that dear old Doctor Grantley.

(Dr. Grantley looks up from paper, sees sofa vacant, looks around disconcerted, encounters Mrs. Coddington.)

MRS. CODDINGTON. — I was about to call to your notice, doctor, this very inter—— *(Bell.)*

DR. GRANTLEY *(cuts her short)*. — I am sure you will be interested, Mrs. Coddington, in what I'm reading here. Pray sit ye down, ma'am. Hum! haw! As I was saying, the Morrison tariff bill which introduced the proposed horizontal reduction ——

MRS. EFFINGHAM. — Horizontal! That means poor Arthur was lying on the ground.

DR. GRANTLEY. — Was stupidity itself; was neither scientific nor practical. *(Recaptures Appleby and Walton.)* I appeal to you, Appleby; to you, Walton. Was it either scientific or practical? *(Brings them down to sit on either side of Mrs. Coddington.)* Hem! haw! While we have been wasting time ——

MRS. EFFINGHAM. — Wasting time! I knew it!

DR. GRANTLEY. — In an idle discussion of its absurdity, the welfare of our country *(raising his voice)* — its *very life* — is trembling in the balance!

MRS. EFFINGHAM. — His life! *(Sinks in chair, L.)*

> *(All turn to her. Mrs. Coddington goes over to back of chair, Walton stands at table; Appleby, R.)*

DR. GRANTLEY. — The heat of the room, no doubt. *(Goes over, feels pulse.)* Oh! it's a trifle; she'll do very well.

> *(Goes back to table, re-seats Appleby and Walton, resumes reading. Bell rings. Enter Thomas; goes back of Mrs. Effingham's chair.)*

THOMAS. — Please, ma'am, it's Misther Rutledge.

> *(Enter Rutledge. Sensation.)*

MRS. EFFINGHAM *(flies to him)*. — Arthur! Not dead; not wounded!

RUTLEDGE. — Neither, that I know of. But, if you would promise to keep this up, I might consent to any fate.

MRS. EFFINGHAM.— Then you killed that poor, poor Captain Hartshorn ?

RUTLEDGE.— I left him a moment since, yawning his head off at the club. He may be dead by now, for he was reading my Uncle Grantley's pamphlet.

DR. GRANTLEY.— Eh! What's that? He couldn't be doing a more admirable thing.

MRS. EFFINGHAM.— Then what does it mean? All of us are burning with curiosity to hear the true story of your duel.

RUTLEDGE.— Duel! What duel?

DR. GRANTLEY.— Nobody told me anything about a duel.

ALL.— Yes, tell us about your duel!

APPLEBY.— Y-y-yes, t-t-t-tell us ——

RUTLEDGE.— Duel! My good friends, you flatter me. I have n't the least idea, nor ever had, of fighting with anybody, thank you. Just now — *(glance at Mrs. E.)* — a lamb might lead me at its own sweet will.

ALL.— Then there has been no duel?

RUTLEDGE.— Certainly not.

MRS. EFFINGHAM *(tenderly).*— But, oh, had you known how we have suffered on your account. Have n't we, Mr. Walton?

WALTON.— Acutely. Especially Grayson, who has gone to collect your dying sentences.   *(Enter Thomas.)*

THOMAS.— General Sabretache!

(Enter Sabretache.)

SABRETACHE.— Ladies, your most obedient! Grayson tells me the news of this duel has reached you. No doubt you are astonished I did not mention it. The fact is, I was pledged to secrecy. But for circumstances I need not mention, I was to have been Hartshorn's second.

(Enter Thomas.)

THOMAS.— Misthress Marabout.

(Enter Mrs. Marabout.)

MRS. MARABOUT *(out of breath).*— My dear Lilian, I've just run in again to say the story of the duel was a hoax. Rutledge dined at Delmonico's last night, lunched at the club at two, was in the bow-window at half-past, and is at this moment driving Fanny Golightly down the Avenue in his dog-cart.

(Bell.)

THOMAS *(announcing).*— Misther Grayson!

GRAYSON.— My dear Mrs. Effingham, I'm told, on the best authority, Dr. Grantley has just paid all of Rutledge's debts, and that he and Miss Golightly are to be married a fortnight from to-day.

RUTLEDGE *(advances from behind Mrs. E.).*— Thanks, thanks, very much, my friends. So kind of you to settle my affairs. Certainly I am to be married very soon, but not — *(takes Mrs. E.'s hand)* — to Miss Golightly.

> *(All bow, and congratulate Mrs. E. and Rutledge. Sabretache, Grayson, and Mrs. Marabout retire up, disgusted.)*

MRS. CODDINGTON.— Well, I declare, I won't get a wink of sleep to-night unless I find out how this story got about. Who started it?

ALL.— Who could have started it?

APPLEBY.— W-w-w-w-who c-c-c-could ——

MRS. EFFINGHAM.— Perhaps Miss Coddington can enlighten us.

ARABELLA *(jumps violently.)* — I?

MRS. CODDINGTON.— Oh! Ah! I remember. I shall expire!

MRS. EFFINGHAM. — Come, Miss Coddington, speak up. Who told you about the duel?

ARABELLA *(bursting into tears).*— Nobody. I made it up. It wasn't my fault, mamma. You know you told me on no account to let the conversation flag.

> *(Sensation, surprise and laughter.)*

MRS. CODDINGTON. — Oh, I am disgraced! Wait till I get you home, miss. Dr. Grantley, may I offer you a seat in my carriage?

DR. GRANTLEY *(who is talking to Walton and Appleby).* — No, thank you, ma'am; I am very much engaged.

MRS. CODDINGTON. — Perhaps you'll stop to dine with us? I'm sure Mr. Coddington would be charmed to have a talk with you about the tariff.

DR. GRANTLEY. — Ah, in that case, madam — *(Offers her his arm.)* And I say, Walton, I'll meet you later at the club, and finish what I was saying. Oh, I'll wait for you, never fear. *(They retire up.)*

WALTON. — Come, Appleby, Grayson. Let us fall into line, and retreat from the field with drums beating and with colors flying.

MRS. MARABOUT *(to Walton).* — Going back to your buffaloes and Indians for consolation, I presume.

WALTON. — Not when I can derive such entertainment from nature nearer home, Mrs. Marabout.

(Mrs. M. tosses head, turns head away.)

RUTLEDGE *(to Walton).* — Stay for the wedding, won't you?

MRS. EFFINGHAM. — Stop, please. I hope nobody will go until I've thanked our friends for their kind attendance on our Tea at Four o'Clock.

Curtain.

TWO STRINGS TO HER BOW

A COMEDY IN TWO ACTS
ADAPTED FROM THE FRENCH

———

CHARACTERS:

DUMESNIL,	*A bourgeois father.*
MME. DUMESNIL,	*His wife.*
COUDRAY,	*The friend of the family.*
ALPHONSE DE LUCEVAL,	*Suitor of Cécile.*
CÉCILE,	*Dumesnil's daughter.*
BAPTISTE,	*An old servant.*

———

TIME: BEGINNING OF XIX. CENTURY
SCENE I: THE PARLOR OF DUMESNIL'S COUNTRY HOUSE
SCENE II: THE GARDEN OF DUMESNIL'S COUNTRY HOUSE

Two Strings to Her Bow was first given at Sedgwick Hall, Lenox, September 27th, 1884 — and again at the Lyceum Theatre in New York, as part of a programme for the benefit of the Babies' Shelter of the Church of the Holy Communion, on the afternoon of April 7th, 1887. The costumes used on both occasions were of the Empire period of France. It will be observed that the play offers an opportunity for both songs and dances at the finale of second act; but that they can, with propriety, be omitted. The scene with Cécile at piano in the first act can be enlarged or omitted altogether.

The cast of this play at the Lyceum Theatre was as follows:

MONSIEUR DUMESNIL ....*Mr. Henry Gallup Paine.*
MADAME DUMESNIL...................*Miss Ada Webster Ward.*
CÉCILE ....*Miss Alice Lawrence.*
ALPHONSE DE LUCEVAL ....*Mr. Edward Fales Coward.*
MONSIEUR COUDRAY ....*Mr. Alfred Young.*
BAPTISTE ....*Mr. Harold Harrison.*

      Stage-Manager..... ....MR. DAVID BELASCO.

TWO STRINGS TO HER BOW.

ACT FIRST.

(A room in a French country house of the middle class; C. B. a folding-door; doors R. and L. To the left of the audience a table, guitar or piano, flowers, and music books; to the right a table with embroidery, etc., mantel mirror, clock, and vases. Monsieur Dumesnil in his dressing-gown; Madame Dumesnil, a stout lady, in camisole and curl-papers.)

DUMESNIL.—If you would only take pattern by me, my dear. Don't hurry yourself; keep cool and comfortable. Our visitor can't possibly arrive before ten o'clock.

MADAME DUMESNIL *(moving about fussily)*.—Don't hurry myself, Monsieur Dumesnil! Pray, what would become of this house if I did n't hurry myself? And to-day, of all days!

DUMESNIL.—Too much care killed the cat. Perhaps Monsieur de Luceval will like us better without so much ceremony.

MADAME DUMESNIL.— I should think you might trust matters to me, Monsieur Dumesnil — I, who have seen the world. Did n't I once go to the ball at the Mayoralty and dance with his Honor in the opening set ? Here I am, on the point of marrying off my only daughter — in the act, as it were, of embracing my future son-in-law. Dear boy, how I love him already! How I like to think of the young couple! What an interest I shall take in their affairs!

DUMESNIL *(taking snuff).*— No doubt, no doubt. You 'd be a new kind of mother-in-law if you did n't. But don't count your chickens before they are hatched, old lady. Our son-in-law, heaven bless him, has to pass upon us first, to say whether he will accept us. He is handsome, young, an orphan, of domestic tastes,— rich ——

MADAME DUMESNIL *(interrupting).*— Rich ! An orphan ! Dear creature, my heart expands more and more to him !

DUMESNIL *(as before).*— Tired of the heartless routine of fashionable Paris, he has determined on settling in the country. He has bought the chateau whose turrets we see yonder from our south window ——

MADAME DUMESNIL *(sits, eagerly).*— Such a house! Such furniture! Such a farm and poultry yard! Cécile will be a great lady. Oh, I can see them walking arm-in-arm from church, and all the people staring and crowding to see my girl. Husband, I shall certainly get some of Cécile's guinea-eggs. I suppose we shall dine there every other Sunday. Dear young man ! He must be sweet-tempered ! How he will enjoy his seven little brothers ! Such gay, lively children as ours are. I fancy the dear creatures will be forever at their house. One thing worries me dreadfully, Dumesnil. Do you think our son-in-law would like tomato sauce, or spinach with his cutlets ?

DUMESNIL.— Softly, softly, wife ; wait till our bird is safely in the cage. You women are always so impatient.

(Voice of Coudray, heard outside, C. B.) — No need to stable him, my good man. Just walk him up and down in the shade a bit; I 've but a moment to stay.

DUMESNIL.— That 's Coudray, our dear girl's godfather. What a piece of luck that he should have returned to-day, to hear our news.

MADAME DUMESNIL.— Yes, and how surprised he will be to know we have secured such an excellent match for Cécile, without his help. For a year past Coudray has made it his business to drum up all the desirable marrying men.

COUDRAY *(entering, C. B., riding-dress and whip. Salutes Madame D., then D.).*— Here I am, glad enough to get back to the fields and woods, I 'll warrant you. Good news flies fast, you know, and I 've traveled full speed.

> *(D. and Madame D. seize each one of Coudray's hands, and speak alternately with great rapidity.)*

DUMESNIL.— I knew you would sympathize with us, old fellow.

MADAME DUMESNIL.— One can always count upon Coudray!

DUMESNIL.— In character and position unexceptionable.

MADAME DUMESNIL.— The fortune is better than we expected!

DUMESNIL.— His ideas about a settlement most liberal!

MADAME DUMESNIL *(takes steps).*— I can fancy you dancing at the wedding, Coudray. Ha! ha!

DUMESNIL *(takes steps).*— Yes, how Coudray will cut the pigeon wing. Ha! ha!

> *(Coudray, C., is more and more surprised. He looks from one to the other.)*

COUDRAY.— The mischief knows how you two have found me out. 'T was only this morning we settled it, De Géronville and I; and I 've been in the saddle ever since.

DUMESNIL *(surprised).*— What!

COUDRAY.—Hark ye, Dumesnil, you remember when we were boys together, how all our dreams of the future were of becoming millionaires. I was to be a bandit, you a corsair. We were to amass money, and marry princesses. Ho! ho!

DUMESNIL *(poking him in ribs).*—Yes, and to live in palaces, and eat off gold and silver plate. Ho! ho!

COUDRAY.—Here we are, two grizzled old fellows; you married to a jolly soul who has given you a houseful of boys and a girl. I am a rusty old bachelor. We have about money enough to rub along with. What interest have I but you and yours? My little bit of money will go to Cécile when I die. She is my godchild, and my pet. Ever since she approached the marriageable age I have been plotting and planning to secure for her a worthy husband and a good establishment. At last, my friends, I have succeeded. To-day, thank fortune, our girl is provided for!

MONSIEUR AND MADAME DUMESNIL *(together).*— She is! But how did you find it out?

COUDRAY.— How did *you* find it out, you mean. As you know, I am never so zealous as when serving a friend. Another man might have bungled in so delicate a mission; I— never! The principal object of my stay in town was to bring to a successful issue the matter I have long had in mind. The husband I am empowered to offer you for Cécile is no less a person than the son of our Inspector-General, Monsieur Jules de Géronville!

MONSIEUR AND MADAME DUMESNIL.—Monsieur Jules de Géronville! Impossible!

COUDRAY.—In proof of it, I bring you the formal letter of demand from his father. What luck, Dumesnil! The Chief of your Bureau, the man who holds your fortune in the hollow of his hand. You are a made man, and our dear Cécile has a charming husband. Why, what does this mean? You hesitate, you draw away from me! *Coudray has made a blunder!*

DUMESNIL.—You mistake us, Coudray. My best of friends, you never were more mistaken. Astonished—bewildered, we may be, but not insensible. *(They embrace, kissing on both cheeks.)*

COUDRAY.—Why in the devil, then, are you so backward in welcoming Cécile's husband?

DUMESNIL.—I'm not at all backward, I assure you. The difficulty is, what can she do with two of them?

COUDRAY.—Two of them!

MADAME DUMESNIL *(sits).*—Yes, my dear Coudray; when you arrived we were in the very act of preparing our household to receive a visit from our other son-in-law. I mean Cécile's first husband—that is—really, I seem to get a little mixed. How very unfortunate she should have to miss being the daughter-in-law of our Inspector-General. To be sure *(sighs)*—an orphan son-in-law is always more desirable. This poor De Luceval is quite alone in the world—no inconvenient mother and jealous sisters; then the De Géronvilles have always held themselves so very high—it really is perplexing.

COUDRAY *(whistles).*—Alphonse de Luceval! So *this* is your boasted prize! A conceited cockney, who has come down here from Paris with a little money in his pocket, bought out the land adjoining yours, and thinks to impose on us honest country folk by his fine city airs and graces. Put a little whipper-snapper of a fellow like that beside my big, handsome, manly, sensible Pierre de Géronville! Bah! the idea's preposterous.

DUMESNIL *(angrily).*—Coudray!

COUDRAY *(walking about whipping his boots with riding-stick).*—Of course, it is none of my affair. I've no right to take exception. Cécile is your child, not mine. Be as ridiculous as you please.

DUMESNIL.— Much obliged to you, Monsieur Coudray. Certainly, Cécile is my child, as you obligingly concede; and I propose to dispose of her hand without reference to the impertinent remonstrance of an outsider. *(Angrily.)* What! my word is passed, and you compel me to retract it? Bah! the man has lost his wits.

> *(As Coudray, in great indignation,— seizes his hat, lifts his whip with a gesture of defiance, and starts to leave the room, the voice of Cécile is heard in the garden outside.)*

CÉCILE.— Yes, that's my godfather's horse. I was sure of it. I am almost as happy when he comes back to us as when papa does. I'll pick a rose for his nice old button-hole. There's his favorite bush. Dear, dear godpapa!

> *(During her speech Coudray and Dumesnil waver toward and from each other. At the close of it their hands meet in a friendly clasp.)*

DUMESNIL.— Coudray, my dear old fellow, what a fool I was to be angry!

COUDRAY.— No, Dumesnil; I was the idiot. My unfortunate testy temper!

DUMESNIL.— You know I never can help boiling over.

CÓUDRAY.— Say no more about it. I accept De Luceval.

MADAME DUMESNIL *(wiping her eyes).*— This is as it should be. It seems it is next to impossible to take both of Cécile's suitors *(sighs deeply)*, and we must make the best of circumstances.

> *(Cécile is heard singing without. A song may be introduced here, or not.)*

DUMESNIL.— Here she comes! Let me warn you both to say nothing that will lead her to suspect a suitor is in question.

MADAME DUMESNIL *(disappointed).*—Not tell her about her sweet young man, who's coming to be her husband! Why, Dumesnil, who ever heard of such unfatherly behavior!

DUMESNIL.— Never mind, wife; I have passed my word to Monsieur de Luceval. He has taken a fancy to appear among us unknown to Cécile, save in the light of a purchaser for my south meadow.

COUDRAY *(aside).*— Hum! So our young cockney is romantic, it appears.

> *(Enter Cécile. She is dressed in white, with wide straw hat. She has a basket of eggs in her hand, and holds a bunch of roses, which she distributes.)*

CÉCILE.— One for you, godpapa *(kisses him on both cheeks)*, to welcome you home again; one for mamma, and this deep-red beauty for my father. Do you know, to gather it, I had to shake out a bee — a great, big, saucy fellow! After a hard struggle, I conquered him.

COUDRAY *(taking from breast-pocket a case).*— Fair exchange is no robbery, Cécile. See what I found for you in the Rue de la Paix.

> *(Cécile opens case and takes out a bracelet. She utters a cry of delight, and kisses Coudray's hand.)*

CÉCILE.— Godpapa, you are a darling! I never had anything half so lovely before. *(Tries it on her arm before mantel mirror.)* Nobody knows how long I have been sighing for a bracelet! *(Admires her arm in various postures.)*

DUMESNIL *(examines basket, which she has placed on chair).*— And what have we here, little vanity?

CÉCILE.— Those — ah! take care, papa — those are the eggs I found just now in the hay.

MADAME DUMESNIL *(aside).*— Innocent little dear! Such, such is life. Little does she know that these very eggs will make an omelette for her future husband.

CÉCILE.— It was such fun! When I was tired, the farmer's wife gave me a great bowl of milk and a slice of her good brown bread. How hungry I was! And how I devoured it!

MADAME DUMESNIL *(aside).*— How providential that she should have taken the edge off that unromantic appetite. I can never teach Cécile that a well-brought-up young woman must always appear indifferent to her food.

CÉCILE.— And so, having eaten heartily, mamma, I am going to ask to be excused till dinner-time. I have ordered the pony to be saddled, and, with old Jean to attend me, I'm off for a long, delightful ride in the forest.

MADAME DUMESNIL *(aside).*— Bounce out of the house at the very moment her lover sets foot in it! *(Sharply.)* You will do nothing of the kind. Think of your complexion, after a ride in heat like this. Besides, the dressmaker has just sent home your new gown, and I wish you to try it on. Go to your room at once, and put on that gown without delay.

CÉCILE *(pouting).*— I can't endure new gowns. A stiff, tight thing with a long, tiresome tail to it. How much better I can run and jump in one like this.

> *(Works her arms and shoulders, and goes through gymnastic exercises like a schoolgirl.)*

DUMESNIL.— Obey your mother, my child. *(Exit Cécile, reluctantly.)* And this, Coudray, is our future Madame de Luceval! But see, time is flying, and I am not dressed to receive my son-in-law. Of course you'll stay, Coudray. Smoke your cigarette on the terrace, whilst my wife and I make ready for our guest.

> *(Exeunt Dumesnil and Coudray. Madame Dumesnil is about to go to her room, when she discovers something awry in the furniture. She sets to re-arranging it, when Baptiste enters.)*

BAPTISTE.— Madame, madame!

MADAME DUMESNIL.— Well, Baptiste?

BAPTISTE.— Monsieur is in the greatest way! He can't find his embroidered waistcoat anywhere.

MADAME DUMESNIL.— That's just like Dumesnil. Can't

see an inch before his nose, when I put his things all together on a chair not ten minutes since.

BAPTISTE.—And madame, madame, the cook wants to know if she shall serve the kidneys and the cutlets together; and madame has forgotten to tell me what table-linen to use.

MADAME DUMESNIL.— I am almost distracted. The clover-leaf set, of course, you booby; they are lying in your pantry. And send Marie to me.

(Voice of Dumesnil, R.)

DUMESNIL.—Madame Dumesnil, my dear, I can't find my blue necktie anywhere.

MADAME DUMESNIL *(clapping her hands to her ears, runs out)*.—Coming, coming, Monsieur Dumesnil. Oh, what a piece of work to marry off one's daughter.

(Exit Baptiste, L. Exit Madame D., R. As her mother disappears, enter Cécile, C., with fingers on her lips.)

CÉCILE.— To marry off one's daughter! *I* am a daughter. I am the only daughter here, and so it must mean me. What a perfectly dreadful thing! When one is married one has a double chin; one has to be always fussing with the cook, or dusting the furniture, or counting the linen from the wash, or disputing with papa about whether or not the beef is overdone. Mamma has n't a bit of fun, *ever*. Fancy her riding races on the pony, or climbing haystacks, or hunting eggs. If I am to be married ——

(Enter Baptiste; comes up to his young lady with affectionate familiarity.)

BAPTISTE.—Come, Mademoiselle Cécile, that is n't at all the face I should have hoped to see on my young lady the day she expects her future husband.

CÉCILE *(starts violently)*. — Husband! Oh, I never thought of him. Oh, dear Baptiste, must there be a husband?

BAPTISTE.—Well, mademoiselle, it 's in general to be expected when a young lady sets out for to get married.

Cheer up, mademoiselle, and don't look so down in the mouth. We *(assumes an air of importance)* — your honored father and mother, and your godfather, and all of us — have spared no pains to bring about this happy moment. The young gentleman we have selected is one worthy of the family, and will reflect credit on our choice. It is your duty to do everything you can to make a favorable impression on him. In an affair of this kind, you know, mademoiselle, there is always a risk that the suitor may withdraw.

CÉCILE.— Withdraw !

BAPTISTE.—Yes; make himself scarce — back out, you know.

CÉCILE.—Oh, if he only would! Tell me, Baptiste, you dear, kind Baptiste, how one might set about making the suitor — back out, you know ?

BAPTISTE *(with dignity).*—Tut, tut, tut, my little lady! My master does me the honor to repose confidence in his old Baptiste, and shall I prove faithless to the trust ? Besides, Mademoiselle Cécile, not only does the credit of the family demand that you should be married, and have an establishment of your own, but there is another reason.

CÉCILE *(mournfully).*—Tell me all — all at once, Baptiste !

BAPTISTE.—My young lady is no doubt aware that I have been for many years in her father's service, and that during that time my reputation for sobriety has extended wherever the name of Baptiste is known. *(Waves his arms.)*

CÉCILE.— Yes, of course. Don't be so slow, Baptiste.

BAPTISTE.— My reputation for strict temperance has not only brought upon me the scoffs of outsiders, but has been the cause of a coolness between me and my oldest comrades. Now, to retrieve my name for good fellowship, I owe them some amends. I have made a solemn vow that, on the day your marriage is decided, I will indulge myself to the extent of — well — of putting an enemy to my lips to steal away my wits. *(Dumb show of drinking.)* I hope my good young lady will remember how *much* depends on her. *(Bell rings, C. B. Baptiste looks back.)* There he is! There's the future husband! Run, Mademoiselle Cécile, and get on your finery, as madame bids you.

CÉCILE *(shades eyes with hand and looks out).* — A young man on horseback at the lodge gate. At any rate, he's neither fat, nor bald — like husbands generally.

> *(Bell inside rings ; Dumesnil's voice, L.)*

DUMESNIL. — Baptiste, Baptiste !

BAPTISTE *(shrugs).* — There's my master calling! *(He does not stir.)*

> *(Bell inside rings ; Madame Dumesnil's voice, R.)*

MADAME DUMESNIL. — Baptiste, Baptiste !

BAPTISTE *(shrugs).* — There's my mistress. Curious how they always do it together. *(Does not stir.)*

CÉCILE *(desperately).* — Oh, it's all over with me ! Why must I have a husband ?

> *(She runs out, C. B. Madame Dumesnil runs through door, R. She is in an ample dressing-gown ; holds curling-tongs in hand, and has a large curl-paper on top.)*

MADAME DUMESNIL. — Baptiste, you stupid fellow, run and open the door without delay. *(As Baptiste goes out, he looks at audience.)*

BAPTISTE. — I can hardly believe my good luck. The happy day has come. After years of abstinence — only a beggarly glass of absinthe on Sundays! Put it to yourselves! *(He makes motion of drinking, smacks lips, and exit, C. B.)*

MADAME DUMESNIL. — Hurry, hurry, Baptiste. Where in the world is my husband ? Monsieur Dumesnil, Monsieur Dumesnil! Oh, he ought to be there to receive the dear young man.

DUMESNIL (*rushing in, L., without coat, and brandishing two hair-brushes*).— Wife, wife, he 's come! No mistake about it. He is riding up the front gravel at this moment.

MADAME DUMESNIL (*sharply*).— And are you going to be dancing a fandango with those hair-brushes all day? and not a soul ready to do the honors of the house. That is the way. You are always behindhand in every important crisis.

DUMESNIL.— I was busy with Coudray. We had to compose the letter turning off the other suitor; and diplomacy takes time, I tell you.

MADAME DUMESNIL (*regretfully*).— True, that letter had to be written. Being forced to refuse the son of the Inspector-General is the only drawback of this happy day! But hurry, Dumesnil, hurry.

DUMESNIL.— I can't. My coat is not yet brushed.

MADAME DUMESNIL.— You surely don't expect me to receive my son-in-law like this!

(*Enter Coudray.*)

DUMESNIL.— Here 's Coudray, just in the nick of time. He is the very man. Coudray, my dear fellow, hasten to do the honors to Monsieur de Luceval for us. You have just the air of dignified repose — in addition to the fact of having on your coat. (*Pushes Coudray to door.*)

MADAME DUMESNIL.— Yes, do, Monsieur Coudray. Your hair is not in curl-papers.

(*Exit Coudray.*)

There, he is off — and so am I.

DUMESNIL.— And I.

(*Retires, brushing his hair wrong. As he passes Madame Dumesnil they collide. She burns him with tongs accidentally; he jumps in the air, etc., etc. Exeunt Monsieur and Madame Dumesnil, R. Enter Coudray, ushering in Alphonse de Luceval, C. B.*)

COUDRAY (*stiffly*).— I am charged, sir, by my friend, Monsieur Dumesnil, with the duty of receiving you in his

stead. Madame Dumesnil and himself will join us immediately.

DE LUCEVAL *(aside)*.— Immensely cordial old party.
(Aloud.) You are too kind, sir. A member of the family,
I presume ? Great-uncle,— grandfather,— hey ?

COUDRAY *(stiffly)*.— Not at all, sir ; not at all. *(Aside.)*
Too cool, by half. What right has he got to presume anything ? *(Aloud.)* I am an old and intimate friend of the
Dumesnil family, and godfather to the young person
whom ——

DE LUCEVAL.— Ah ! Godfather to the young person
whom ——, are you ? *(Aside.)* Well, I can see for myself
that I have no especial favor to expect from the godfather
to the young person whom —— *(Aloud.)* Very good
friend, you have no idea what pleasure your honest rustic
countenance gives me. It is a sort of assurance that all
the rest will be in keeping.

COUDRAY *(aside)*.— Honest rustic countenance ! Confound him for a city popinjay ! *(Aloud.)* I don't know what
your expectations are, sir, but I assure you that ours ——

DE LUCEVAL.— Oh, I won't trouble you with the list,
worthy godfather. Let me confide in you my emotions.
Just now, as I rode up the avenue, I said to myself, "There,
behind those modest green blinds, is the companion of my
future joys and sorrows, a dear little unsophisticated innocent, with a skin like cream and hair like sunbeams ; for I've
seen her at mass, two Sundays since. And then those good,
simple bourgeois, her parents ; no pretensions, no state, no
ceremony. They will come forward to receive me with
honest hands, wide open, and the girl will have no accomplishments, no frills and flounces —" By the way, what
has become of the family ?

COUDRAY *(aside)*.— What a very abrupt young man.
(Aloud.) Monsieur and Madame Dumesnil are at their
toilet, sir.

DE LUCEVAL.— Toilet!

COUDRAY (*pompously*).— Yes; and I am glad of this opportunity to tell you that my friend Dumesnil is entirely worthy of all you say of him. During the forty years of our intimate friendship I have never known him to neglect a duty, or withdraw from his word when he had passed it. His daughter is a young person whose merits will develop daily as she advances in years. Pious and modest, of excellent principles, we have taken pains to bestow on her, from earliest childhood, a due measure of feminine accomplishments — to bestow on her a distaste for the mere fripperies of life — to bestow on her ——

DE LUCEVAL (*aside*).—While they were about it, why did n't they bestow on her another godfather? What an alarming list of virtues! My enthusiasm is quenched already. (*Aloud.*) My good sir, you alarm me. I don't want a district visitor.

COUDRAY (*aside*).— A district visitor!

DE LUCEVAL.— I want a sweetheart, not a missionary.

COUDRAY (*aside*).—A sweetheart! I'm not so sure of his principles after all.

> (*Enter Madame Dumesnil in full toilet, with a portentous cap, and Dumesnil in knee-breeches, buckles, his chapeau under his arm ; behind them Cécile, awkward in a stiff new dress, her eyes cast down, her hair puffed outrageously, etc. As they come in, the most absurd and exaggerated exchange of salutations takes place. No one will ever allow the other's bow or curtsey to be the last.*)

DE LUCEVAL (*aside*).— Good Heavens! This is interminable. One might as well be dancing a perpetual minuet.

MADAME DUMESNIL (*aside*). Cécile, come forward, child, and don't hide in my pocket.

DUMESNIL (*to his wife, aside*).—Say something, can't you? Deuce take it, if I can find a word. Women are always ready with their tongues.

MADAME DUMESNIL *(aside)*.— I 'm frightened to death. I have n't an idea in my head.

> *(The parents and Cécile advance in a stiff row.)*

DE LUCEVAL.— I owe you, ladies, a thousand apologies for disturbing you so early in the day.

MADAME DUMESNIL *(with an assumption of society ease)*.— Not at all, monsieur. My daughter and I are apt to be a little lazy, that is all. Nothing ages a woman so soon as early rising, they say; and we owe it to society to preserve our complexions.

DE LUCEVAL *(aside)*.— Hers is like a lobster. *(Aloud.)* There are some complexions, madame, that time only touches to improve.

DUMESNIL *(with assumed elegance)*.—It is we who owe you an apology, my dear sir, for keeping you waiting, and for allowing you to surprise us in this demi-toilette.

COUDRAY *(aside)*.— Demi-toilette! What does he mean? He 's not been so fine before since his own wedding-day.

MADAME DUMESNIL *(same manner)*.— But the country covers a multitude of sins against etiquette, for which, you must know, we are the most determined advocates. *(Aside.)* Cécile, step forward, and hold your head up!

CÉCILE *(aside)*.— I can't, mamma; this dress pinches me so.

DE LUCEVAL *(looks at Cécile, aside)*.— What abominable hair-dressing. It makes a fright of her!

MADAME DUMESNIL *(to husband, aside)*.— See how he looks at her! There is rapture in his gaze.

DE LUCEVAL *(still looking at Cécile, aside)*.— This is a most unpleasant surprise. A little, stiff, commonplace, ill-dressed, boarding-school miss, in place of my woodland nymph.

DUMESNIL *(aside to his wife)*.— For goodness' sake, make the girl talk. She has n't said a word. Everything depends upon first impressions.

MADAME DUMESNIL *(aside to him)*.—And the trouble generally is to make her hold her tongue. *(Aside to Cécile.)* Come, come, my dear; speak up, without delay.

CÉCILE *(half sobbing)*.—I can't possibly, mamma. I'm laced too tight.

DUMESNIL *(aside to Coudray)*.—Do you keep up the conversation, Coudray! As the godfather and family friend it is your business. *(Wipes his brow.)* This is the hardest day's work I ever did.

COUDRAY *(aside)*.—There is justice in what he says. I clearly am the person to rescue all parties from the embarrassment of the present situation. Let me think of a remark that is applicable under all circumstances to a newly arrived visitor. Ah, I have it. *(Steps forward. Aloud to De Luceval.)* What, sir, are your impressions of our neighborhood?

DE LUCEVAL *(aside)*.—Is he reporter, as well as godfather? *(Aloud.)* Very fair, indeed. Good natural points, certainly *(glances at Cécile)*, but spoiled by an attempt at cultivation ignorantly bestowed.

COUDRAY.— Hum! I suppose you are a trifle bored by your solitary life at the chateau?

DE LUCEVAL.—Not at all. I am never bored when I have the company of my own thoughts.

MADAME DUMESNIL.— You are exactly like my daughter here, I do declare. Oftentimes I ask her if she would not prefer the society of some gay young people to her books; but no, it is impossible to wean her from those serious occupations.

CÉCILE *(aside)*.— Oh, pray, mamma, be quiet about me.

COUDRAY *(aside)*.— Slow work, this. *(Aloud to De Luceval.)* Perhaps you play the flute?

DE LUCEVAL *(laughing)*.—So badly that I reserve the accomplishment entirely for myself.

MADAME DUMESNIL.— That's exactly like my daughter.

I 'm always urging her to play and sing in company, after the mints of money that have been spent on her music ; but she persists in saying that my husband and her brothers are the only persons who can appreciate her fairly. (*Cécile disappears behind her mother.*)

COUDRAY (*aside*).— See how I 've set the ball a-rolling. (*Aloud.*) No doubt you draw, Monsieur de Luceval ?

DE LUCEVAL.— I am afraid I am destitute of all the polite accomplishments, Monsieur Coudray.

MADAME DUMESNIL.— Oh, you should just see the beautiful head of Romulus my daughter has drawn. She brought it home from school with her ; and, actually, when it was taken out of the portfolio she did n't know it herself.

CÉCILE (*from behind her mother*).— None of us girls ever knew our things, mamma, after the drawing teacher touched them up !

MADAME DUMESNIL.— Run, fetch your portfolio, my dear, and let Monsieur de Luceval see your head of Romulus.

CÉCILE.— I can't, mamma. He was such an old fright we nailed him on the barn door as a target for our arrows !

DE LUCEVAL (*laughing, aside*).— Here 's one touch of nature, by Jove !

MADAME DUMESNIL (*reproachfully*).— For shame, Cécile. At any rate, you shall sing for Monsieur de Luceval. By a happy chance the man came to tune your piano this morning, and here is the last song from the new opera.

DE LUCEVAL.— Yes, mademoiselle ; you are surely not unkind enough to deny me this rare musical treat ?

(*Cécile attempts to sing ; business at piano.*)

CÉCILE (*aside*).— He is making fun of me ! I am ready to cry ! I am crying ! Oh, dear ! oh, dear ! oh, dear !

(*She bursts into tears and escapes from the room. Coudray follows Cécile, while Monsieur and Madame Dumesnil apologize in dumb show to De Luceval, who stands bowing with an air of mockery.*)

MADAME DUMESNIL *(aside, fanning herself).* — Nothing goes right.

(Enter Baptiste with a napkin beneath his arm.)

DUMESNIL *(aside).* — Ah! here is Baptiste to announce breakfast. How lucky. At least, if the young man can't draw, or play, or sing — he can eat.

BAPTISTE *(bowing).* — The breakfast is served, madame.

DUMESNIL *(bowing).* — I hope that Monsieur de Luceval will share our family meal.

MADAME DUMESNIL. — A simple country meal, monsieur.

BAPTISTE. — And cook says if the company don't make haste her omelette will fall as flat as any pancake.

MADAME DUMESNIL *(angrily, aside).* — Be quiet, you awkward idiot.

DE LUCEVAL. — Really, my kind neighbors, it is hardly worth while. I merely called — I dropped in to talk over affairs — that little meadow through which my brook takes a turn, Monsieur Dumesnil; perhaps you will be willing to part with the land; another day we will discuss it. *(Offers to go.)*

MADAME DUMESNIL *(holds up her hands, aside).* — Only a little meadow. Would anybody believe it? *(Aloud.)* But you can never think of leaving us like this, neighbor De Luceval, and the breakfast smoking on the table?

DE LUCEVAL. — Thanks, very much; but the truth is I've already breakfasted.

MADAME DUMESNIL. — Already breakfasted!

DE LUCEVAL. — A cup of fresh milk this morning at the farm.

MADAME DUMESNIL. — That's exactly like my daughter. Such sweetly simple tastes. Cécile! *(Calling Cécile.)*

COUDRAY *(re-entering).* — I am sorry to say that Cécile begs to be excused. The little witch has coaxed me until I don't know my right hand from my left, to say she may stay in the garden till we have finished breakfasting.

MADAME DUMESNIL *(catching at idea).* — Perhaps Monsieur de Luceval would like, also, to remain in the fresh air awhile.

DE LUCEVAL *(indifferently).* — As you like. If Monsieur Dumesnil does n't object, I 'll take a look at his pigs.

> *(He bows, and goes out, C. B. Madame Dumesnil aghast.)*

MADAME DUMESNIL. — Pigs!

COUDRAY. — Come, come to breakfast, my friends. For breakfast one must, whether the course of true love runs smooth or no.

MADAME DUMESNIL *(aside).* — And all my good things wasted on Dumesnil and old Coudray!

> *(Coudray offers his arm to Madame Dumesnil, who accepts, with look over shoulder at door, C. B. Dumesnil follows.)*

Curtain.

ACT SECOND.

A garden, with rustic bench in arbor, R. Enter Cécile in ordinary dress, knitting-bag on arm.

CÉCILE. — I saw him going down the lilac walk, and I hid behind the bushes till he passed. Hateful, conceited creature! I know he was laughing in his sleeve at us. *(Goes into arbor.)*

> *(Enter De Luceval. Cécile takes knitting out of bag and begins to work.)*

DE LUCEVAL. — I saw her steal away from me, and followed her. Something tempts me to make one last effort. Perhaps she is not the affected, brainless doll she seems to be! Ah! there she is, without her finery. What an improvement. *(To Cécile.)* It appears we have been playing a game of hide and seek, mademoiselle.

CÉCILE *(with assumed stupidity)*. Hum. *(She drops the ball of wool, L.)*

DE LUCEVAL *(picking up ball, and restoring it with a bow)*.— They tell me that you, like myself, have breakfasted, *al fresco?*

CÉCILE *(stares vacantly)*.— Al — what? I don't understand you, monsieur. *(Drops ball again, R.)*

DE LUCEVAL *(picks it up, etc.)*.— I should congratulate myself on the result.

CÉCILE.— Yes? *(Drops ball again, C.)*

DE LUCEVAL *(picks it up, aside)*.— Devil take it! *(Aloud.)* Since it has secured for me this opportunity to profit by the conversation of a young lady who is as clever as she is beautiful.

CÉCILE *(with a movement of anger, aside)*. — Now he is ridiculing me. Horrid thing! *(Aloud, stupidly.)* If you please, monsieur, did you wish to see the pigs?

    (She drops the ball, which rolls out, back. She stands motioning him to follow it.)

DE LUCEVAL *(aside, in disgust)*. — Confound it, the girl seems an absolute idiot. Can it be she means to make a fool of me? *(Picks up ball. Aloud.)* For the last time, mademoiselle. *(He bows and attempts exit, R.)*

CÉCILE *(laughing)*.—The other way to the pigs, monsieur.
                              (Exit De Luceval, angrily, L.)

CÉCILE.— Victory! Victory! We fairly hate each other.
                              (Enter Madame Dumesnil.)

MADAME DUMESNIL. — I hope Baptiste will remember to — Baptiste! *(Enter Baptiste.)* Put the sherry in the cupboard, and take that claret stain out of the cloth before you fold it. *(Exit Baptiste.)* These servants are so stupid. Ah! how tired I am. This dress is so uncomfortable.

Everything goes wrong to-day. Cécile, I thought Monsieur de Luceval was with you.

CÉCILE (*demurely*).— Monsieur de Luceval preferred the pigs, mamma.

MADAME DUMESNIL.— And how dare you let him prefer the pigs ?

CÉCILE.— Never mind, mamma ; it is better so. We should always have been quarreling. You know you and papa say " anything for a quiet life."

MADAME DUMESNIL.— What do you mean, you saucy girl ? Oh, you have all combined to drive me mad to-day.

(*Enter Coudray.*)

COUDRAY.— Well, Madame Dumesnil, our little game is up.

MADAME DUMESNIL (*agitated*).— Speak quickly, Coudray. Don't keep me in suspense.

COUDRAY.— De Luceval has backed out, confound him ! (*Cécile, back, waves her handkerchief.*) He's been expressing his regrets in such flowery terms that I can't remember half of it. But the main point is, he's off, or will be as soon as his horse is saddled.

CÉCILE (*claps hands*).— Joy ! joy ! Come, mamma, don't take it so to heart. This is the first time I've felt happy since I have heard the name De Luceval. (*Exit, back.*)

MADAME DUMESNIL (*sinks upon bench*). — Ungrateful wretch ! What have I done to deserve this blow ? Oh, I shall die of vexation.

COUDRAY.— Cheer up ! Remember you've another string to your bow — the son of the Inspector-General.

MADAME DUMESNIL (*brightening*).— That dear De Géronville ! I always said he would suit Cécile the best.

(*Enter Dumesnil, an open letter in his hand.*)

DUMESNIL (*rubbing his hands*).— You will say I have lost no time. I'll show that jackanapes De Luceval that we can be independent of him. Here is my letter to the In-spector-General accepting for my daughter the honor of his son's hand in marriage.

MADAME DUMESNIL.—I hope there 'll be no mistake this time, husband.

DUMESNIL.— Mistake! Read that, madame. *(Hands letter.)* It 's as plain as pen and ink can make it — as plain as the nose on your face, Madame Dumesnil. Read that, Coudray!

(Goes back calling, " Baptiste! Baptiste! ")

COUDRAY *(takes letter from Madame Dumesnil).*—Very good, very good. Make hay while the sun shines, and strike while the iron 's hot. No doubt the young man will be here to-day.

MADAME DUMESNIL.—To-day! I wish they would give me a little time between my sons-in-law. Poor Cécile's first husband can hardly be past the gate. However, — for my child's sake —— *(Fans herself.)*

(Enter Baptiste.)

DUMESNIL.— Baptiste, you will carry this letter with your own hands to the house of the Inspector-General, and fetch an answer. Be very careful, and lose no time to go and come. Remember that your young lady's marriage depends on you!

BAPTISTE.— Begging your pardon, sir,— if it is not taking too much liberty,— is this really and truly the day of my young lady's betrothal?

DUMESNIL *(pushing him).*— Really and truly, my good Baptiste. Here is a piece of money with which to drink her health. Oh, I forgot you are such a temperance man; put it into your pipe and smoke it — only do be quick.

BAPTISTE *(pockets money, aside).*—He little knows my vow! *(Aloud.)* By the way, sir, the other one is outside, asking the honor to take leave of monsieur and madame.

DUMESNIL.—The other one!

BAPTISTE.— Yes, sir; the one we are not going to marry. But he can wait, can't he, sir?

DUMESNIL.— Ask the gentleman to step here, and be off with you, rascal.

(Exit Baptiste, shows in De Luceval, exit again.)

DE LUCEVAL *(advances with a frank and manly air).*— My dear Monsieur Dumesnil, I was not content to take leave of you without another word of apology. I am deeply sensible ——

DUMESNIL *(who has regained his natural manner).*— Say no more, neighbor. The whole affair was a mistake. We are plain country folk. I don't wonder you found us not up to your notions.

DE LUCEVAL *(embarrassed).*— May I beg you to believe ——

DUMESNIL.— Never mind, never mind. You don't understand what an affair it is among us bourgeois to marry off an only daughter. We were a little off our balance, that is all. Now it is over, thank Providence, we are free to act like our every-day selves again, without any nonsense or ceremony. Make yourself at home here, Monsieur de Luceval, now and when you will.

DE LUCEVAL *(aside).*— This is quite another man. *(Aloud.)* I am more than pleased to accept your friendship, Monsieur Dumesnil. *(They shake hands.)*

DUMESNIL.— Then stay to dinner with us.

MADAME DUMESNIL.— Yes, do, Monsieur de Luceval.

DE LUCEVAL *(aside).*— What an extraordinary change of base! And what nice, unaffected people they are! *(Aloud.)* It's a great temptation, in exchange for my solitary table.

DUMESNIL.— Agreed, then. You'll like our home-raised mutton! Besides, my boy, you can help us, if you will. You are a man of the world; we are blundering country folk who spoil whatever matters of diplomacy we touch. We have on hand another affair of importance; a little enterprise — like yours, you understand.

De Luceval.—What, the deuce! Another suitor for the hand of mademoiselle?

Dumesnil.— Why not? He was only waiting till you had had your turn. One of these days when you have a daughter to marry off, you will understand the situation. This time we must be quite sure not to fall into any mistake like the first one. The new young man is in every way desirable for Cécile.

De Luceval *(aside, winces).*— I wish him joy of her. *(Aloud.)* I congratulate you, Monsieur Dumesnil. Count upon my services.

Dumesnil.— Thank you. And as to the little meadow you spoke of, it is yours at your own price.

De Luceval.—This is really kind. If I accept, 't is more through sentiment than for any other reason. I wished to own that bit of land, because I have learned that just there once stood the little house where my Uncle Rambert lived in his boyhood.

Coudray.— Rambert — Paul Rambert, who was the captain of a merchant vessel, your uncle? Why, Rambert was my chum at school, and the best fellow in the world. Have you never heard him speak of Louis Coudray?

De Luceval.— Of course I have, many a time. He swore by old Coudray, as he called you.

Coudray *(jovially).*— Give me your hand, my boy, for Rambert's sake. Of course, his sister married a De Luceval. What a donkey I was not to have thought of it! I was at your christening. ha, ha, ha! but perhaps you would hardly remember it. What has come of my wits that I did n't recognize Rambert's nephew? But you 've changed a good deal since then, to be sure. I may have seemed cold to you at first, but you must n't mind it. As Dumesnil says, we were none of us ourselves.

De Luceval.— You must make it up by coming to Luce-val on all occasions. You will not refuse to shoot over my woods?

Coudray *(delighted).*— The best shooting in the country! This is heaping coals of fire on my head. I wonder I did n't notice what a fine, manly face he has.

De Luceval.— You will both dine with me on Sunday, I trust. I can give you some capital Burgundy, and my cook is a treasure, in his way.

Coudray.— A chef! What an admirable young man Rambert's nephew turns out to be!

Dumesnil.— And now, since we understand each other, away with ceremony. I am off to attend to matters on the farm, and you, Coudray, must come with me. My wife has her housekeeping to look after. We treat you like one of the family, De Luceval. Make yourself at home. Help your-self to books, pencils, music. Walk in the garden, stroll in the orchard, read, sleep. This is Liberty Hall. We 'll meet at dinner-time. *(They go out, arm in arm.)*

De Luceval *(takes up book from table).*— What a fool one is to judge by first impressions. And I was going off in disgust of these worthy people! How came they ever to have such a little idiot for a daughter? Ah! here she comes. *(Grimace of distaste.)*

Cécile *(coming in with basket of flowers).*— Ah — I beg your pardon. I thought my mother ——

De Luceval.— I can understand, mademoiselle, that my continued presence here surprises you.

Cécile *(frankly).*— Not at all, monsieur. My father tells me that you have promised, like a good neighbor, to stay for dinner. I am glad you have proved your generosity.

De Luceval.— My generosity, mademoiselle?

Cécile *(smiling).*— Yes, in forgiving the annoyance we caused you this morning.

DE LUCEVAL *(bows).*—Mademoiselle. *(Aside.)* Now that she knows I have refused her, what a scrape I 'm in. *(Aloud.)* I beg you to believe — that reasons — reasons — strictly personal reasons ——

CÉCILE *(aside).*—What fun! He is as ill at ease as I was. Ha, ha, ha! *(Aloud.)* Don't be alarmed, monsieur. I will not hold you to account. My god-father has bid me make a friend of you ; and now that I know you don't wish to marry me — I really don't think you so *very* ugly and disagreeable. As a proof of it, go on with your reading. I 'll just arrange my flowers.

> *(As she scatters flowers upon the little table De Luceval*
> *follows her with his eyes.)*

CÉCILE.— What! you are not reading ? Your book does n't interest you ?

DE LUCEVAL.— Passably. But, if you don't mind, I think I had rather talk.

CÉCILE.— As you please. I have nothing else to do.

DE LUCEVAL *(aside).*— Small encouragement. *(Aloud.)* Then, as you are in a listening mood, perhaps I may explain some things in my manner, this morning, that may have displeased you.

CÉCILE *(with sudden spirit).*— Some things ! Everything. You assumed such a scornful, mocking air when you came near me — you affected to belong to a superior order of beings — to look down on my good parents, my honest godfather. How could a girl of spirit submit to patronage ? The idea of marrying you filled me with dismay. I thanked heaven when you withdrew your suit.

DE LUCEVAL *(mortified).*— If we were all to judge by appearances, mademoiselle ——

CÉCILE *(arranges her roses, rapidly).*— Ah! I know what you would insinuate, monsieur. But here we are, on the verge of a quarrel, when my godfather has given me the strictest orders to make friends with you. Tell me about the uncle whose memory is so dear to him.

DE LUCEVAL.—Willingly, for my uncle Rambert was the saint to whom I owe all the good in my life. He was the captain of a vessel, who had spent more than thirty years in active service. Rich in honors and ripe in years, he died recently, bequeathing to me not only his fortune, which was considerable, but an example of virtue it shall be the effort of my life to follow.

(Cécile drops her flowers on table, and gazes at him fixedly.)

DE LUCEVAL.—It was his wish that I should give up Paris, and settle in the country. By good fortune I heard of the estate adjoining yours, and was able to purchase it. The meadow your father has been good enough to part with to me, once contained the little cottage where my uncle was born. Do you wonder that the spot is sacred to me—that I dreamed of attaching myself to it by another link?

CÉCILE *(faintly)*.—Would that, too, have been his wish, monsieur?

DE LUCEVAL.—It was the last he expressed to me. That I should choose for my wife a country girl, true and loving, coming of good bourgeois stock, and inheriting their simple virtues. When I found myself alone in the Chateau Luceval, I was oppressed with its size, with my solitude. My park was like a desert. My servants were strangers, and my days hung heavy on my hands. The smoke curling from the chimneys of your home seemed an invitation. I saw you at church. I made inquiries about your parents, and heard of them and you what filled me with hope. This is my uncle's choice, I said, and it is mine. *(He draws near. Cécile's head droops. Enter Coudray.)*

COUDRAY.— Well, young people, and how do you get on? Cécile, I am asked by your mother to bid you prepare the dessert. No doubt Monsieur de Géronville also will be here to dinner.

CÉCILE *(starts).*—Monsieur de Géronville!

COUDRAY.— Yes; your future husband. Has n't my friend De Luceval been helping us in that direction as he promised?

DE LUCEVAL *(coldly).*—I — I had forgotten, Monsieur Coudray.

COUDRAY.— By this time Baptiste has placed in the hands of the Inspector-General your father's letter of acceptance to his son.

CÉCILE.—Monsieur de Géronville m — my — future husband! Oh, no, no, no, I cannot!

> *(She bursts into tears and runs off. As Cécile goes out in tears, her father comes in, back. He looks curiously at her, then at De Luceval, then waits, back, during the following interview.)*

COUDRAY.—Tut, tut, tut, what does this mean?

DE LUCEVAL *(walks back and forth agitated).* — Tell me, Monsieur Coudray. You were my uncle's friend; that means you are my friend, does it not?

COUDRAY *(giving him his hand).*—Trust me, my boy.

DE LUCEVAL.— Promise that you will not despise me for a weathercock. Lend me your aid. I am desperately in love with Mademoiselle Cécile. The first glance of sympathy from her eyes revealed her to me. She is the wife I need. The wife I *will have!* I want you to ask her for me from her father.

COUDRAY.— Ask for her — again — after — Whew!!!

DE LUCEVAL.— Yes, that is exactly what I want.

COUDRAY.—" What I want "—" what I want!" Listen to his majesty! Why, you young turnabout, the thing 's impossible. They have already accepted Monsieur de Géronville.

DE LUCEVAL.— Let them break with him.

COUDRAY.— Impossible. In this case there are graver reasons. Such a rupture would bring ruin to my good friend Dumesnil. His chief dependence is his income from the Registry Bureau; and of this the Inspector-General, a proud and insolent man, may deprive him at any moment.

DE LUCEVAL *(joyfully).*— If that 's all, I invite you to my wedding on the spot. Fortune? Thank Heaven, I have enough for both.

DUMESNIL *(comes forward with dignity).*— Pardon me, my friend, if I heard what has just passed. No, Monsieur de Luceval, my word to De Géronville is given, and it cannot be retracted. Fortune you may have, but not enough to cover the dishonor of a broken pledge.

COUDRAY *(strikes Dumesnil on the back approvingly).*— Right, as usual, my friend. What did I tell you, De Luceval? Be reasonable, give up this fancy. You may be best man at her wedding yet.

> *(Enter Madame Dumesnil followed by Cécile, whose eyes are downcast.)*

MADAME DUMESNIL.— Such a pleasant surprise. Some of Cécile's young friends have heard the news, and are coming to wish her joy. Well, what cheerful faces! One would think a funeral instead of a wedding is in prospect. What! it can't be that Monsieur de Géronville, too, has — *(She totters and falls into a chair.)*

DUMESNIL *(dryly).*— Be comforted, my dear. Our present difficulty is a superfluity of suitors.

DE LUCEVAL *(seizing Madame Dumesnil's hand).* — Ah, madame, speak for me! Urge him to retract his promise to De Géronville. I love your daughter, and I promise to make her happy.

MADAME DUMESNIL.— There you go again. Just as I had got accustomed to my other son-in-law! Really, my head is so confused I don't know what to say.

> *(Dumesnil and Coudray talk to her in dumb show.)*

DE LUCEVAL *(to Cécile).*— Mademoiselle, I appeal to you. You have pardoned my blindness, my fatuity. Add to your goodness by believing in my love.

CÉCILE *(sadly).*— You are too late, monsieur; and even if I believed, my father's word is passed. That is the law of this household.

DE LUCEVAL.— At least, tell me that I might have hoped — that you are not in love with this man they have chosen for you?

CÉCILE.— Alas! no, monsieur. I have only seen him once — and besides — I have never even known what love might be — until to-day.

DE LUCEVAL *(impulsively).*— Cécile!

> *(Cécile glides past him to her father. Dumesnil extends his arms. Cécile hides her head on his breast, weeping. Coudray turns away and takes snuff to conceal emotion.)*

DUMESNIL *(holds out disengaged hand to De Luceval).*— Monsieur, I had asked you to spend the evening here. After what has passed I think you will agree with me that it is wiser for your visits to be suspended for the present. You are a man — be strong for yourself — for me, and — for this poor child. *(He kisses Cécile's hair.)*

DE LUCEVAL *(with resolution).*— You are right, Monsieur Dumesnil, and you shall see me no more. Farewell, madame. Farewell, Cécile — forever ——

CÉCILE *(impetuously).*— Oh, not forever — don't say that. — My father is so good, so loving, he will find some way — No, he cannot. Oh, father, father! *(She falls again, sobbing, into Dumesnil's arms.)*

> *(Enter Baptiste, pale and dishevelled. He falls on his knees at Dumesnil's feet.)*

BAPTISTE.— My good master, I deserve to be kicked out of the house like a dog.

DUMESNIL. — What have you done, rascal?

BAPTISTE.— It is what I have n't done, monsieur. Monsieur knows that I long since made myself a promise to get drunk on the day when my young lady's marriage should be decided — the first time in my life, monsieur, I swear by all the saints.

DUMESNIL.— Well, well, go on.

BAPTISTE.— After drinking with some old comrades, I fell asleep on the bench before the tavern door. When I woke up, a few minutes ago, I said to myself, " Baptiste, an errand was intrusted to you — an errand on which depends the wedding of your young mistress. What have you done with the letter to Monsieur Géronville ? "

DE LUCEVAL *(joyfully)*.— Great Heaven ! Was it lost !

BAPTISTE.— Monsieur, not at all ——

COUDRAY.— You delivered it ?

BAPTISTE.— Oh, dear ! no, monsieur ; not at all ——

DUMESNIL.— Speak up, then, fellow. What did you do with it ?

BAPTISTE.— Messieurs ! Madame ! Mademoiselle ! I shall never have courage to own my guilt ; but here *(produces a soiled and crumpled letter)* is the letter to Monsieur de Géronville.

DE LUCEVAL *(seizes Baptiste violently by the hand and shakes it)*.— My good man, you are our benefactor forever. Take this. *(Gives him money.)*

COUDRAY.— Baptiste, you are a capital fellow, and worth your weight in gold ! Take this ! *(Gives him money.)*

DUMESNIL.— Baptiste, you have served me long and faithfully. Consider your wages raised from this day forth.

MADAME DUMESNIL *(in melancholy tone)*.— I wish I could understand it. As far as I can see, I 'm to have *no* son-in-law.

BAPTISTE *(feels pockets)*.— No more do I understand it, madame — I, that expected to be dismissed upon the spot.

(Aside.) Now that I see how satisfactory it is to all parties, I wish I 'd had another drink. The truth is, it was n't possible. *(Baptiste retires, up stage.)*

DUMESNIL *(tearing the letter and throwing it away).* — And now, De Luceval, with all my heart, I give to you my daughter.

CÉCILE *(archly).* — And with all *my* heart, papa.

(De Luceval kisses Cécile's hand, they retire up.)

MADAME DUMESNIL *(embracing her husband effusively).* — How well you 've managed, husband, dear! I always liked dear De Luceval the best. To be sure, poor De Géronville was a splendid match.

COUDRAY *(rubbing his hands joyfully).* — Dumesnil, your hands are full; suppose I go and draw up the new letter to the Inspector-General? Tact, hey? Diplomacy? I 'm the man for your little business, hey?

DUMESNIL. — Do so, Coudray, and tell him ——

MADAME DUMESNIL *(interrupting).* — Be sure you are *very* considerate, Coudray. Make him understand how much we regret ——

CÉCILE. — But we don't a bit, mamma.

DE LUCEVAL *(bows).* — Pray, madame ——

MADAME DUMESNIL. — I beg your pardon, son-in-law. You know it is our duty to be very civil to those De Géronvilles.

DE LUCEVAL. — Never mind that, mother-in-law! Tell him, Coudray, that he shall have the De Luceval support in the matter he wrote me of. That will make all smooth between our families. And now, to celebrate this happy day, here come the young people of the village to do honor to their favorite.

(Enter young girls in procession, song, dance, ending in country dance, in which principals join. Last of all, Baptiste is imprisoned in a ring of girls and made to dance.)

Curtain.

www.ingramcontent.com/pod-product-compliance
Lightning Source LLC
Chambersburg PA
CBHW031158050726
47495CB00019B/2476